PUFFIN BOOKS

ATOMIC SWARM

Jason Bradbury likes gadgets – a lot! He has scoured the globe to find them and rarely stops talking and writing about them. He also likes computer games – perhaps even loves them. The first computer game he ever played consisted of nothing more than two dots and a straight line, but it was enough to ignite a lifelong passion for the (pixellated) pastime – and, despite having real *human* children and a robot called Vernon to look after, Jason still finds time for more game playing than is wise.

He is best known as host of Five's *The Gadget Show*, on which he swims with sharks, rides rocket-powered bicycles and jumps off bridges – but before his TV career took off he has been a comedian, a script writer and a breakdancer.

Jason lives in London, where he cruises the streets on various electric vehicles and newfangled types of skateboard.

The science and technology in the Dot.Robot series is real and Jason has witnessed much of it first hand – including a trip in a self-driving robotic car in Las Vegas, a flying robot test flight and a look at an invisible jacket . . . if you can look at something that's *invisible*.

To find out what Jason is up to, go to his website *www.jasonbradbury.com*

JASON BRADBURY

DOT.ROBOT
ATOMIC SWARM

PUFFIN

For Mum

PUFFIN BOOKS

Published by the Penguin Group
Penguin Books Ltd, 80 Strand, London WC2R 0RL, England
Penguin Group (USA) Inc., 375 Hudson Street, New York, New York 10014, USA
Penguin Group (Canada), 90 Eglinton Avenue East, Suite 700, Toronto, Ontario, Canada M4P 2Y3
(a division of Pearson Penguin Canada Inc.)
Penguin Ireland, 25 St Stephen's Green, Dublin 2, Ireland (a division of Penguin Books Ltd)
Penguin Group (Australia), 250 Camberwell Road, Camberwell, Victoria 3124, Australia
(a division of Pearson Australia Group Pty Ltd)
Penguin Books India Pvt Ltd, 11 Community Centre, Panchsheel Park, New Delhi – 110 017, India
Penguin Group (NZ), 67 Apollo Drive, Rosedale, North Shore 0632, New Zealand
(a division of Pearson New Zealand Ltd)
Penguin Books (South Africa) (Pty) Ltd, 24 Sturdee Avenue, Rosebank,
Johannesburg 2196, South Africa

Penguin Books Ltd, Registered Offices: 80 Strand, London WC2R 0RL, England

puffinbooks.com

First published 2010
1

Copyright © Jason Bradbury, 2010
All rights reserved

The moral right of the author has been asserted

Set in Absara OT Light 11.5/17 pt
Typeset by Palimpsest Book Production Limited, Grangemouth, Stirlingshire
Made and printed in England by Clays Ltd, St Ives plc

British Library Cataloguing in Publication Data
A CIP catalogue record for this book is available from the British Library

ISBN: 978-0-141-32396-1

www.greenpenguin.co.uk

Penguin Books is committed to a sustainable future
for our business, our readers and our planet.
The book in your hands is made from paper
certified by the Forest Stewardship Council.

Paraguay

Asunción, the capital of Paraguay, wasn't called the 'cheapest city in the world' for nothing. But that didn't mean that Fabie, the fifteen-year-old waiter at the Cafe Cassava, could afford to eat more than one main meal a day. If the tourists tipped, then he might be able to pick up a burger and Coke for one US dollar on the way home to Barrio San Pablo.

It had been a hot day, even by Paraguayan standards, hot enough to turn the asphalt sticky, and this meant Cafe Cassava had been busy all day. The ice machine had broken down, as was the case every other week, and Fabie had added hourly trips to find ice to his already hectic day. Consequently, Fabie missed the tips from several customers.

Fabie was thankful at least for the impressive tower of the hospital that overshadowed the whole piazza. It made Cassava the city's coolest place to eat and drink when the sun was at its most merciless. The soaring structure also provided a steady flow of Paraguay's richest citizens, two of whom had just sat down in Fabie's section.

'Good morning, gentlemen,' Fabie said. He could tell immediately that the two men were English speakers. 'Would you like to start with a cold drink?'

'You betcha,' said one of the men, a bronzed American with a thick neck and large biceps bulging beneath his T-shirt. 'I'll have a cold beer and a large bottle of mineral water. And make sure it's the real deal. Not tap water and superglue!'

The man was referring to the practice adopted in bars and cafes throughout the city of filling old plastic bottles with tap water, then glueing their tops back on and selling them to tourists as new. The shelves in Cafe Cassava's own kitchen were stocked with hundreds of the counterfeit bottles.

'That doesn't happen here, sir,' Fabie lied.

'And for you, sir?' he continued, turning to the most smartly dressed customer he had seen all week. Something about the man was familiar. The man was dressed in a cream-coloured suit. He wore a pale-blue shirt with a crisp collar and a white-and-gold striped tie. It was knotted almost up to his neck – a quintessentially English style of dress and quite something in this heat.

He looked up at the young waiter from beneath the

brim of a panama hat and asked for a *yerba maté* in perfect Spanish.

Fabie was taken aback. Not only did the Englishman speak excellent Spanish but he had asked for a drink usually only ordered by locals. Interesting.

As Fabie added hot water to the powdery mixture of brewed herbs the Englishman had ordered, he suddenly remembered when he'd seen the customer before. It must have been about a year ago. For several weeks he'd been a regular customer. But it wasn't the man's face Fabie remembered because most of that had been conspicuously concealed behind bandages. (Fabie had assumed this was the result of plastic surgery treatment, for which the hospital was famous throughout South America.) No, it was the man's dapper dress and flamboyant mannerisms that had initially jogged his memory. But what Fabie now gleefully recalled above all those things was that the man had been the most generous tipper he, or any of the other waiters, had ever met.

Fabie let out a yelp of excitement. He'd be eating burgers all week!

While the American examined his water bottle's plastic lid for signs of tampering, the Englishman took a sip from the metal straw poking out from the bowl of hot, dark liquid that Fabie had placed in front of him.

'*Bueno!*' he exclaimed.

Fabie glowed at the compliment. This was surely a

good sign. 'It's hot to be drinking *maté*,' Fabie added chattily, hoping to increase his chances of a generous tip. It was strange talking to someone whose face you couldn't see, though. The man's hat covered most of his forehead and beneath that was a large pair of black sunglasses.

'There is a theory that Indians drink hot tea on a hot day to cool themselves down,' the Englishman replied, looking up at him. 'Something to do with the dilation of blood vessels. Personally, I chose your delicious infusion because I like the taste.'

Fabie just stopped himself in time from taking a sharp intake of breath. The man's skin ran in deep ripples across his face, almost as if it had been melted. Fabie wondered for a moment what might have happened to him – he couldn't imagine this had been the work of any plastic surgeons that he'd heard mentioned by the wealthy people around here. But really this was none of his business. His concern was getting that tip. So, instead, Fabie politely enquired after the men's intention to stay for lunch. 'The beef soup is excellent today.'

'Not today,' said the Englishman.

Fabie's heart sank. If the men were only drinking, there would be no generous tip.

'Perhaps I can get you some cornbread and olives?' he offered, desperate to salvage something from this.

'Whatever,' the American said, dismissing the waiter. A disappointed Fabie walked back towards the kitchen.

He placed a bowl of olives on a plate and surrounded it with several slices of *sopa Paraguaya* cornbread. He stepped back on the terrace to make his last attempt at securing a tip that day, when there was an enormous explosion.

The young waiter instinctively threw himself to the ground as a wall of dust raced across the piazza, engulfing the cafe terrace.

The wail of car alarms filled the air, quickly followed by voices of men and women calling to see if colleagues and loved ones were OK. Fabie couldn't see more than ten metres or so ahead, the dust was so thick. But eventually, as it cleared, he looked up to see that where the tall hospital building had stood for the past few years, blocking out the sun's harsh rays, there was now only blue sky. Through the chaos and dust, the two men he had been serving walked towards him. The muscular American walked straight past Fabie, but the Englishman stopped and glanced down at the young waiter lying flat on the ground.

Putting a hand inside his jacket, he pulled out a large brown leather wallet. He took a hundred-dollar note from inside it and, squatting down, handed it to Fabie.

'That *maté* was excellent, by the way.'

CHAPTER 1

Smack!

Jackson Farley's eyes widened. He could feel the blood start to pump a painful beat in his temple.

This was it. Certain death. No matter what numbers the brilliant young mathematician could crunch and regardless of the powerful robots he could summon with a mere wave of his mobile phone, there was nothing the thirteen-year-old could do now to prevent his certain demise.

This chess match was lost.

Jackson tried to rub away the tension in his head that another defeat had brought. He looked at the face of the young opponent who was sitting on the other side of the chessboard. Atticus79 had just slammed his last chess piece down with the force of a gladiator delivering his final killer blow. Now he sat there on the grass, grinning.

'That's what I love about you Brits,' said the tall, skinny fourteen-year-old. 'You bring all your ideas over here, and us Americans end up doing them better. American football, that's rugby, but better. And you guys claim you invented the sandwich, but the American sub is way better! Now this?'

Atticus79 was referring to Bullet Chess, an entire chess game played within just sixty seconds. Jackson had introduced it to him several months ago and today Atticus79 had won all of the ten matches they'd played.

'Mind you, I suspect my victory might have something to do with the fact that you're playing two games simultaneously!' Atticus79 pointed at the thin rectangular tablet computer that Jackson was balancing on his knees.

'What, *Whisper*?' said Jackson. 'I'm not really playing it. It's more work than play.'

Jackson had been logged into the online role-playing game for the entire time they'd been playing Bullet Chess. But, as far as he was concerned, guiding his character, WizardZombie, through a few menial tasks could hardly be considered distracting. He'd been playing the game for as long as he could remember. He could do it with his eyes shut.

'What d'you mean, *work*?' asked Atticus79.

'I direct my character, WizardZombie, to mine for gold, do a little blacksmithing here and there, and buy and sell weapons and other goods. After a few hours' play I can usually make enough *Whisper* gold coins to trade them for real dollars on various websites. It's called gold farming – trading game money for real-world money. It helps me supplement my college fees!'

MIT wasn't cheap. Just over a year ago when Jackson had been offered the chance to leave his rather ordinary secondary school in Peckham for a scholarship at the USA's top technology university, the Massachusetts Institute of Technology in Boston, he had been torn. He had desperately wanted to go, but found it very hard to leave his dad.

It wasn't that his dad couldn't cook or keep the flat in order without him or even that they were together all the time – they weren't. What with Jackson being at school in the day and his dad working nights, some days they'd only see each other for a few minutes. But they were a team; they'd been through a lot together. When Jackson's mum had died several years ago and his dad had struggled to keep a job, they'd supported each other.

Mr Farley, however, had given Jackson no choice. 'It's the kind of education your mother and I could never have afforded for you,' he'd said. 'You're going, and that's an end of it.'

As for the cost of moving to America and paying tens of thousands of dollars' worth of college fees, his dad did his best. But it helped that the robotic engineering course, on which Jackson had enrolled, was headed up by J.P. English, the millionaire father of Jackson's fellow roboteer Brooke English, with whom he'd been through so much in the last year.

So here he was, sitting on the lawn in front of MIT's

imposing Great Dome, starting the eleventh chess game of the day, which this time he had no intention of losing to Atticus79. Jackson looked at his chess buddy in between rapidly exchanged chess moves. Atticus79 was tall for his age, made even taller by a thick tangle of wildly curly carrot-coloured hair that shot up and out in all directions. He had the obligatory metal brace glistening between his teeth that so many American teens wore and he was wearing a T-shirt that read 'I ♥ ROCKS'.

It was a joke that only made sense if you knew that Atticus79 was a complete geology nut.

Atticus79 had been one of the first people he'd met during orientation week nine months ago. It had been hard enough that Jackson was abroad for the first time in his life, not even on holiday, but actually living on his own, 5,500 kilometres away from his dad. In those first few strange days, when every fire-engine siren and every pedestrian crossing seemed like it belonged on an alien planet, Jackson was pleased to have found the MIT chess club and in it his new friend, Atticus79.

The two boys were the odd ones out. Both were a lot younger than the ten or so other club members. When Atticus79 had introduced himself with a number in his name, Jackson was immediately intrigued.

'Why 79?' he'd enquired.

'Why do you think?' asked the boy, his brace glinting as he smiled.

Jackson thought for a moment. 'I dunno. Your mum and dad really liked prime numbers?'

In fact, it had been nothing to do with Jackson's favourite mathematical idiosyncrasy. This was all geological. As a young boy, Atticus was obsessed with rocks. While other children in his home state of California were playing hide-and-seek and riding their bikes, Atticus was panning for gold in the streams of his once famous gold-rush hometown. At the age of eight, he found his first sizeable nugget and started a mini gold rush of his own. When a teacher at school named him Atticus79, '79' being the atomic number of gold, the name stuck.

But not even a geology genius, with ten games of Bullet Chess under his belt, was unbeatable.

'Aha!' Jackson let out a long-awaited victory cry.

'No! How did you do that?' Atticus79 didn't even attempt to hide his irritation at losing the chess game. Jackson's killer combination of moves had worked – ten games to one.

'The king must be safeguarded in the opening of a game. You left him open for my rook. Winning makes you cocky!' That was a phrase his dad used. His dad wasn't clever, not like Jackson was, or like his mathematician mum had been, but he had a way of getting straight to the point. Jackson smiled; he would see his dad very soon. It was only three days until he visited for the first time since Jackson had come to America.

Desperate to redeem his form, Atticus79 was already busy setting up their next breakneck bout when Jackson's phone rang from inside his bag.

Jackson flicked it open. 'Hel–'

'Don't panic!' Brooke interrupted.

'Wha–?' Jackson still wasn't given time to finish.

'I may have got myself into another situation.'

CHAPTER 2

'Everybody stay calm!'

From where she was standing at the centre of a multi-car pile-up, Brooke's words could just about be heard above the cacophony of shouting and car horns.

She'd seen it all happen as she was jogging in the park across the street. It would have been hard to miss the driver of the Lamborghini Murciélago SV – rather than wait for the cars in front to move, like everybody else, he'd weaved his way dangerously in and out of the thick line of traffic leaving the city. As soon as he'd seen a gap, he'd opened up the 600-horsepower sports engine and shot forward, only to plough into the back of a tattered old pickup that had pulled up at a pedestrian crossing. At least ten other cars had then ploughed their way into one almighty mess of warped metal and broken glass.

Brooke couldn't see the pickup truck that had taken the full force of the Lamborghini's impact. She'd lost sight of it in the fender-bending mêlée but she knew its driver could be in real trouble. Brooke clambered on to the bonnet of a mangled Chevrolet Camaro and spotted it – an ancient F-Series Ford in baby blue. It had mounted the metal guard rail that ran alongside the Charles River and was now balancing precariously over the edge. Alarmingly, Brooke could see an old man still sitting in the driver seat, wrapped up tight in the wreckage.

She jumped down and ran over to the Ford. 'You OK, sir?' she asked, being careful not to touch or nudge the delicately balanced truck in any way.

'Never been better, missy. I just needs a tow, is all!'

'I think you need to get out of the truck, sir, pretty darned quick!' From where Brooke was standing, the truck looked like it was ready to tip and fall into the river at any second.

'I'd love ta, but this steering wheel is a little close for comfort.'

Brooke leaned over to look through the open driver-side window. The large metal steering wheel was up against the man's chest and it looked to Brooke like the console had been compressed and was pushing down on his legs in the footwell. The truck shifted precariously towards the river, just a couple of metres below.

'Don't worry, sir, I have everything under control.' She checked the time on her phone. 'I should have you out of there in the next five minutes.'

The old man looked surprised at the girl's comment

at first. It was nice of this young slip of a thing to try and say reassuring things, although he couldn't imagine there was much she could do really. But that was fine – it would make it easier for the young girl if he appeared to be comforted by her optimism.

He smiled. 'Well then, I'll just sit back and enjoy the view.'

Brooke turned and surveyed the crash site. The timing of the pile-up couldn't have been worse. It had happened during rush hour and the city was gridlocked. In the far lane, the cars coming out of Boston were rooted to the spot. And the vehicles on the bridge ahead were stacked, bumper to bumper. There was no way the emergency services were going to get through.

Brooke checked her phone one last time.

Running. It wasn't really Jackson's thing. He hated the feeling of blood rushing to parts of his body that were much happier relaxing in front of a computer or a console. But Brooke did sound desperate.

A man trapped in a car. It was just the kind of scenario Brooke and he had talked about and precisely what Brooke's latest robotic creations were designed to deal with. The brilliant mechanical engineer now wanted to use the robots she had previously had to employ in their dealings with MeX – a top-secret robot defence force – for tackling emergencies and helping people.

MeX had been dissolved following the death of Devlin Lear, its creator and famous dot.com billionaire.

Along with the Kojimas, two professional computer-gaming twins from Japan, Jackson and Brooke had both been part of a four-member team, without knowing that Lear was using them as pawns in a multimillion-pound theft. Once they had worked out what he was up to, they'd exposed Lear for the criminal he was. And when he went missing at sea, Jackson had tried his best to put a line under the whole affair and return to his normal life. Brooke, on the other hand, had different ideas and, as usual, had pretty much got her way. It was, in fact, partly how Jackson's move to America had come about. Jackson's scholarship worked for everyone – while he got to study for a prestigious university degree, Brooke and her father had him on hand whenever their projects required some number-crunching.

As the five-storey Metropolitan Storage Warehouse loomed large in front of him, Jackson allowed himself a slow trot. He was in serious danger of coughing up a lung. The enormous dark brown building on the edge of the MIT campus was evocative of a medieval castle. On the side of it, in enormous white letters, were the words 'Fire Proof' – this was also how the building was commonly referred to. It had been built in 1894 to provide secure storage for anyone with something to keep safe from theft, fire and bombing, and its basement was the perfect location for J.P.'s experimental robotics laboratory.

Jackson hurried up to a small side door. As he approached, it opened automatically. The entry system was something Brooke had knocked up – a high-level security lock that used a small laser radar to invisibly scan the unique telltale patterns in a person's heart rate and breathing.

He ran down two flights of steps before entering the lab. It was a huge space, running the entire length of the Fire Proof building, which was about the size of two Olympic-sized swimming pools end to end. Brooke and her father, however, had still managed to fill it. It was crammed with desks, computers and highly complex scientific apparatus. Jackson ran past the section of the lab dedicated to Brooke's mechanic's paraphernalia, where her self-driving car *Tin Lizzie* was caged in an elevator. A few months ago, *Tin Lizzie* had achieved second place in a competition called the X Car Challenge, in which cars had to drive themselves from Las Vegas to Los Angeles. Brooke's robotic car had led the race until suffering a puncture on the outskirts of LA, and she finished just behind the winning car despite driving 30 kilometres with a flat. Brooke had taken the defeat badly and *Tin Lizzie* had sat there gathering dust for some time afterwards.

Beside *Tin Lizzie* was what Jackson had been looking for: a line of stout metal enclosures that ranged along one of the lab's walls like pig pens. Each pen contained a different robot, plugged into an assortment of brightly coloured curly-flex cables.

The first three pens each contained spherical objects about the size of a beach ball, which were held in place by a thick aluminium swing arm. The first pen was reserved for *Punk*. With his twelve sharp spikes retracted, the brushed-metal robot could have been mistaken for a miniature globe – his pockmarks and rough welds representing the planet's oceans and continents. But in fact *Punk*'s hidden prongs packed a real punch.

The sphere in the second pen looked like a giant eyeball. Its surface was pristine gloss white and, on one side, it had a centrally mounted fish-eye lens. The third ball-shaped robot was as perfectly round as the other two, but was bright yellow and criss-crossed with black hazard-warning stripes.

Jackson disconnected several data cables and pipes that were attached to the yellow-and-black robot, then drew a shape in the air with his phone. The motion sensors in the prototype handset, designed by Brooke, recognized the gesture and a virtual keyboard appeared on the phone's smooth plastic surface. Jackson entered a hexadecimal access code and pressed the shimmering red SEND icon.

The sound of compressed air being vented came in four short bursts and the swing arm holding the robot suddenly retracted.

Keeping a tight hold of his handset, Jackson traced a new shape in the air and sections of the robot started to unfold, revealing a series of tightly packed plastic joints, like the segments of an orange. As they slowly unfolded, it became clear that the bulk of the sphere was composed of four mechanical robot hands. Each hand had three fingers and a thumb and was able to extend on an intricate network of intersecting metal ribs, which formed a hub at the centre.

Jackson continued to move his phone freely in the air like a wireless joystick and the machine began to move towards him. After rolling a couple of full revolutions, it extended the fingers of each hand and walked on its fingertips.

Jackson turned his back to the robot and squatted down. He drew a gesture in the air, to which the robot responded by climbing on to his back and wrapping its mechanical claws round his shoulders. Moving the phone carefully now, Jackson felt four pairs of mechanical hands hug him securely, clasping his shoulders and waist until they hung from him like a rucksack.

'I've got *Fist*,' said Jackson into his handset as he grabbed a large raincoat from the back of a chair and struggled to stretch it over the robot on his back.

'Good!' came Brooke's reply through the phone's directional speaker. 'Don't waste any time, amigo! Time's a tickin'!'

*

'Where's that pickup driver?'

A man in a navy pinstriped suit, who Brooke guessed was the driver of the Lamborghini, rushed from wreck to wreck, skittishly puffing on a cigarette. 'Did you see him brake? He's a maniac! How was I supposed to stop?'

'He's trapped in his truck,' said Brooke. She signalled for the man to stop. 'I wouldn't go near him if I were you; it's teetering dangerously on the edge of the river bank.'

'As long as I get his insurance details first, the old fool can drown for all I care!' The enraged man continued to vent his anger, but Brooke was too distracted to listen. A jarring metallic whiff was clinging to the inside of her nostrils – one the young mechanic recognized as the smell of gasoline. She looked down and could see the potentially explosive steel-blue liquid streaming around her running shoes.

'Put that cigarette out!' Brooke shouted in horror at the ranting man next to her.

'Says who?' he replied arrogantly.

Brooke just pointed at the gasoline. 'Put it out now or you'll burn us all alive.'

The man went pale and hurriedly stubbed out his cigarette on a credit card from his pocket. 'You only had to say!'

Brooke ignored him. Time was running out.

Come on, Jackson! Hurry up!

CHAPTER 3

Jackson pedalled hard along the Cambridge streets on his mountain bike, his flapping coat revealing momentary flashes of the strange plastic skeleton wrapped round his back. It was part of his and Brooke's arrangement with J.P. that the robots should never be seen outside the laboratory. The mackintosh was the best Jackson could do.

The bike was a Cannondale Bad Boy, an urban racer with a single 'solo' fork at the front and single-speed gear at the back. A matt jet-black carbon fibre frame, one of the lightest in its class, held it all together. Buying the bike, in his first week in Boston, was why Jackson needed to supplement his college fees by selling the virtual goods he made from playing *Whisper*. He'd had no money ever since, but as the bike swallowed up the road ahead, he knew it was worth it.

As Jackson approached an intersection, he prepared to engage the bike's most impressive feature: an experimental hydrogen fuel cell, designed by Brooke. The cell and hydrogen reservoir were housed inside the frame and produced electricity, which powered a hub at the centre of the back wheel. Just as Jackson was about to push the power button mounted on his handlebars, the lights at the intersection turned red. Jackson considered running the lights, when he noticed two MIT police officers on mountain bikes waiting at them.

He slammed on his brakes and skidded to a stop beside the two officers. They were on tricked-out Specialized mountain bikes. Custom-butted aluminium frames, RockShox and front-mounted police lights and sirens.

'Nice bikes!' said Jackson.

One of the officers nodded from behind his mirrored shades.

'D'you always wear your coat over your knapsack?' said the second cop from behind an identical pair of shades. The flap on Jackson's coat had ridden up and the cop was eyeing what he thought was a section of yellow backpack behind it. 'It makes you look like a hunchback!'

Both cops laughed hysterically.

Jackson needed something to distract them from *Fist*. 'I wish I was allowed blues and twos on my bike,' he blurted out, motioning to the lights and sirens on the police bikes, while furtively reaching behind his back to pull the flap of coat quickly down.

'Why? Are you thinking of riding fast?' asked the second cop sternly.

'Er, no . . . of course not, officer,' Jackson answered nervously.

Just then Brooke's voice blurted out of the phone in Jackson's breast pocket, without even ringing. Jackson had left the handset in push-to-talk mode, which enabled his and Brooke's phones to work like walkie-talkies. 'Where are you?' she shouted.

'I'm getting nearer,' mumbled Jackson self-consciously, aware the two cops were listening in.

'So's my next birthday, tiger, but I need you before then! Get a move on!' came Brooke's loud reply.

'That's my mum!' said Jackson to the cops. 'I'm late for my tea!'

The two cops just stared blankly at him.

Not a moment too soon, Jackson was saved by the change of the lights. The two mounted cops waited for Jackson to move off first and then stayed behind him for what seemed like thirty minutes but was probably more like a painstaking thirty seconds.

Eventually, the police officers peeled away and Jackson turned on to the main road alongside the Charles River. Cars were at a virtual standstill in both directions, so Jackson mounted the kerb. From Brooke's description, she was about two kilometres up.

With the path ahead clear, Jackson pushed the red button Brooke had fitted to his handlebars. There was an audible sigh and a judder from beneath his seat as pressurized hydrogen gas and oxygen, stored in his bike's frame, shot into the cylindrical fuel cell hidden in the down tube. Within microseconds, electric current was flowing to the hub of his back wheel, causing its motor to spin. Jackson could feel the front of the bike lighten as the back wheel tore at the tarmac. The wind whipped his face as his speed rapidly increased. He glanced at the tiny wireless bike computer next to his left hand: 50 kmph! 60 kmph! 85 kmph!

It took him no time at all to reach the crash scene. As Jackson disengaged the hydrogen booster and slowed his bike to a stop, he could see the battered pickup on the edge of the Charles River, its nose hanging over the water. He could also see Brooke with her head inside the car, obviously chatting to the driver.

It was typical Brooke. She had obviously already taken control of the situation, herding the other drivers to the safety of the park across the road, while she and another man tended to the trapped pickup driver. Jackson remembered the first time they'd met in the flesh, when he'd arrived in America. It was certainly unusual to accept an invitation to live and study in a new country with someone you'd never actually been in the same room with. But they had already been through so much together. From different corners of the earth, they'd fought remotely alongside the Kojima twins, as part of MeX, and then stood up to Devlin Lear, exposing his corrupt deeds to the world.

The amazing thing was that all these incredible adventures and life-changing experiences had taken place through means of highly advanced technologies that used the Internet as their communication medium. Brooke, Jackson and the twins had never needed to meet to achieve any of it. But now the two friends shared the same laboratory every day and, despite Brooke's tendency to be moody and extremely bossy, they got on like a house on fire.

'Not a moment too soon,' said Brooke when she spotted Jackson. She immediately walked up to him and began to whisper in his ear. 'Old Man Cooper, the driver of the truck, is trapped in the cabin by his steering wheel. He seems upbeat enough, but there's a doctor with him who told me he suspects things might be a little more serious – he thinks the impact of the wheel on his chest could have caused internal bleeding. And I gotta tell ya, that truck of his is only one slip away from a high dive. We need to get him out of there, pronto!'

Jackson hurriedly pulled off his raincoat, retrieved the phone from his pocket and began to draw in the air the precise movements that he needed *Fist* to make. The doctor looked on, disbelieving, as the spider-like machine on the boy's back responded to these gestures by unfurling and beginning to walk on the fingers of two of his mechanical hands towards the ancient pickup truck.

'What in God's name is that?' the young doctor asked Brooke, cowering behind the truck.

'This is *Fist*,' said Brooke. 'F. I. S. T. That's "Fire, Industry, Security, Tactical" to you. I modelled him on the piston-rod hydraulic spreaders that fire-fighters use to free people trapped in cars. I thought their technology was in need of modernization.'

Looking at Brooke's determined face, Jackson didn't think now was the time to remind Brooke that, on her father's instructions, they needed to be as discreet with *Fist*'s identity as possible. It was bad enough that J.P. would find out about using him in public, even though it was to save the old man.

Fist climbed up the back of the truck and then performed a gravity-defying walk along the truck's side, ending by clinging to the driver-side door, horizontal to the ground.

Jackson carefully manipulated the gestural interface on his phone with two wand-like flourishes, and two of *Fist*'s yellow plastic hands dug in around the hinges and handle of the car door. Gripping the underside and roof of the truck with his two other hands, *Fist* effortlessly ripped off the door. He then walked on to the truck's hood, two hands dropping down through the cavity where the windscreen had been to smoothly peel back the console and steering wheel.

For a moment the pickup truck pitched precariously forward towards the river until *Fist* jumped quickly on to its roof, the weight causing the ancient vehicle to tip back on to the pavement again. Brooke and the doctor wasted no time, pulling the old man to safety through the space where the door had been.

The doctor quickly checked over Mr Cooper and gave him the all clear. But as they walked towards the gathering of drivers at the edge of the park, the pinstriped Lamborghini driver accosted Brooke and the old man.

'So you're the idiot who is going to pay to fix the front of my Lambo!'

'I'm sorry,' stuttered the old man. 'But I don't see how –'

The businessman didn't allow him to finish. 'Thanks to you indiscriminately slamming your old beater's brakes on, you have criminally damaged a four-hundred-and-fifty-thousand-dollar car! I am also late for a very important meeting and I will be billing you for my time.'

'Excuse me?' Brooke interjected furiously. 'Don't worry, Mr Cooper. I saw the whole thing. You were driving at a perfectly steady speed for the conditions. This man clearly can't drive!' she fumed, pointing at Mr Pinstripe.

'Excuse me, little girl, but the adults are talking. Those other sheep might have been content to take orders from you, but not me!'

'That's it! I've had enough of this guy,' said Brooke, glowering at Mr Pinstripe. 'Jackson, give me that phone!'

Brooke walked straight up to Jackson and snatched the

handset from him. She turned to the pickup as *Fist*, now under her control, rose from the bonnet. It was the first time Mr Pinstripe had been quiet since the accident. He just stood, gaping like a goldfish, as Brooke's yellow mechanical creation sprang from the rusty pickup and bounded straight for his sports car, like a dog chasing a bone.

When he reached the metallic purple Lamborghini, *Fist* grasped one of the expensive-looking aluminium wheels with a single plastic hand and ripped it clean off! As *Fist* moved to the roof, the car's owner gasped at the sight of sixteen plastic fingers dancing across the pristine metallic surface to grip all four corners.

'So, are you going to stop bullying nice old Mr Cooper and admit that this accident was caused by your dangerous driving? Or shall I ask *Fist* to rip you a convertible?' Brooke asked sweetly.

The man just nodded.

CHAPTER 4

'Not good!' thundered J.P. as he slammed the phone down. 'That guy, the one whose twenty-thousand-dollar, hand-milled, aluminium racing rim you ripped off, is a lawyer!'

'He's a schmuck!' said Brooke.

'He's a schmuck who is threatening to sue me!' raged J.P.

Back when Brooke and Jackson were members of Devlin Lear's MeX organization, Brooke had hijacked two of her father's prototype mining robots, *Punk* and *Tug*. She was supposed to have provided assistance for a demonstration of the robots in the Mojave Desert to investors. Instead, she had hijacked the machines, and she and Jackson had used them to uncover damning evidence about Lear's criminal operations.

Brooke had come clean with her father about having been duped by Lear into working for MeX. He had forgiven her for stealing his robots, but he would not bend to her demands that they set up their own international robot rescue team, and he made her agree to keep

28

the work they did in the lab completely secret. Brooke, however, was a very determined girl. Only in the last year, she had arranged to have *Punk* and *Tug* shipped back to Boston, restored them both to working order and had also designed and built two new robots, *Tread* and *Fist*. *Tread* was designed as a high-speed pursuit vehicle – a miniature robotic road-traffic cop housed inside a single car wheel, which Brooke hoped police could use to sneak up and neutralize stolen cars and criminals without endangering highway patrolmen and the public with dangerous high-speed chases.

J.P. might have had other ideas, but, as far as Brooke was concerned, *Fist* was a super-strong multipurpose manipulator, designed to rescue anyone from just about anything.

However, the fact that J.P. was already being sued by a bystander of another of Brooke's previous escapades did not help matters. One night, four months ago, Brooke had been alerted to a fire in a university laboratory building, a block from their own lab. When she had arrived at the burning house with *Punk* and *Fist*, a distraught janitor was about to rush into the flames to try to rescue a student trapped in a stairwell. Brooke successfully deployed *Fist* and rescued the girl. But on the robot's way out of the inferno, parts of a window frame it had torn away fell to the ground, causing minor injuries to a few onlookers.

The news headlines that followed – MAD PROFESSOR'S ROBOT RAMPAGE CAUSES FIRESTORM OF DANGEROUS DEBRIS – landed J.P. in deep trouble with the MIT board of governors, not to mention a lawsuit from one of the injured bystanders, which was rumoured to have cost him close to a million dollars.

He'd been mad then, but, having been disobeyed again, he was even madder today. The fact that Brooke had her head down texting as J.P. ranted probably didn't do much to calm him down either.

Jackson, who was sitting at a desk next to Brooke's, was doing his best not to attract J.P.'s attention, a plan which wasn't helped by the fact that his phone kept warming his hand in short pulses. It was something Brooke had named a *thermal alert*. Instead of the vibrations and sounds that standard phones used, Brooke had devised a tiny thermal emitter that could turn the phone hot and cold to indicate incoming text messages and calls. Jackson uncomfortably juggled his phone like a hot potato under his desk, away from J.P.'s gaze, as yet another text arrived from Brooke.

With her feet up on her desk and her hands in her lap, Brooke had been continually texting Jackson her responses to what her father was saying. They read like a running commentary: 'HE DSRVD IT', 'BG DEAL', 'LKE I SAID, SCHMCK!!!' It was her way of giving him space to vent, without answering back.

As J.P.'s rant continued, Jackson sent Brooke his own message: 'U R QCK. U SHUD ENTR TH WRLD TXTNG CHMPN-SHP.' Brooke's reply came back quicker than Jackson imagined was possible. 'I KNW. LST YRS WNNR TOOK 42 SECS 2 TYP TH WNNNG SNTNC.' There was a momentary pause, then another message arrived: 'I CN DO IT IN 35 ;-)'.

Jackson's snigger caught in his throat as J.P. bellowed even louder at Brooke.

'Are you hearing this, young lady? I am seriously considering putting the robots under lock and key, so you can't take them on any more of your misadventures.'

'You'd love that, wouldn't you?' Brooke retorted, suddenly and stubbornly engaging with her father's scolding. 'Lock them up, so they are nice and sparkly for your fund-raising events.'

'You need to get real, Brooke. You were only able to develop *Fist* because of the money I secured from the Defence Advanced Research Projects Agency.'

'Exactly,' said Brooke. 'We could be saving lives with *Fist* – that's what he was designed for, not helping the military to destroy them!'

'Ultimately, he will. But only once the defence industry has had their use of the *Fist* technology, which they paid for!'

'And what about *Verne*?' Brooke spat, jabbing her finger at the white spherical robot that hung on a hook and chain in the robot pens next to *Fist* and *Punk*. 'When you first pitched the idea of an underwater robot, it was to monitor the effects of deep-sea drilling and factory fishing on the underwater ecology. Then you're offered a fat cheque from an oil company and, hey presto, my design brief for *Verne* is to make a sniffer dog for offshore oil prospecting. You sold out, Dad!'

As the argument between father and daughter intensified, Jackson let his attention drift to the rest of the massive underground laboratory. It was a treasure trove of exotic machinery, most of which Jackson still didn't understand after almost a year of working here. As far as he was concerned, J.P. had a point about funding it whichever way he could; the kind of high-end scientific equipment required to fabricate advanced nano-composite materials, or 'smart materials' as the professor called them, didn't come cheap.

Jackson glanced at the robot pens across the lab. *Verne*, J.P.'s own RUV or Remote Underwater Vehicle, was made of a combination of super-strong and super-buoyant syntactic foam and J.P.'s own patented, indestructible plastic, which enabled it to withstand the crushing pressures of the deep sea.

The pen to the left of *Verne* belonged to *Punk*, and on the right was *Fist*. In the next pen was *Tug*, an ultra-strong, high-tensile steel, chisel-shaped flying battering ram. Along with *Punk*, he'd helped Brooke and Jackson fight Lear. At the end of the row lived a robot called *Tread*.

Tread looked just like a spare wheel, but inside his steel hub was cutting-edge technology that included gyro-stabilized ultra high-definition cameras, a side-ejecting barbed-stinger for stopping cars and wirelessly powered taser darts to stun runaway criminals.

The super computers, photonic crystal lasers and scanning electron microscopes required to invent all this were incredibly expensive – even more than a millionaire robot-ics-engineering professor could afford. Without the financial help of corporations and government grants, Brooke's dream of developing emergency robots to help humanity would never be anything more than pure fantasy.

Deep down, of course, Brooke knew this. She just couldn't resist an emergency and a chance to test her technology – and her father couldn't resist reprimanding her for it.

Both, however, stopped arguing pretty quickly when a two-metre-tall giant wearing multicoloured shorts and sandals walked into the room. Father and daughter rushed over to greet Nathaniel Goulman – J.P.'s charismatic laboratory assistant.

The Australian had been the professor's right-hand man, ever since finishing a chemistry PhD five years before. Goulman's passion for chemistry and materials was exceeded only by his love of sailing and he had just returned from a sailing trip around South America.

'Good to have you back, Nathaniel,' said the professor,

shaking his muscular assistant by the hand, the grip he received making him visibly flinch. 'How was your trip?'

'Amazing, mate!' Goulman declared. 'Unfortunately, we didn't encounter pirates. I've always found the idea of defending my yacht against pirates strangely romantic. But South America did yield a couple of pieces of treasure.' He swung a large waterproof sailing bag from behind his back, opened its sealed top and pulled out a couple of objects.

'For you, Brooke!' he said, handing Brooke a crumpled carrier bag. 'And a little something for my English friend too,' he smiled, handing Jackson a parcel wrapped in newspaper.

'I'd hardly describe it as treasure, Ghoul!' laughed Brooke warmly as she unfurled a black T-shirt with MY FRIEND WENT TO RIO AND ALL I GOT WAS THIS LOUSY T-SHIRT written on it. 'Once I've ripped the arms off and put a few tears in it, it'll be more my style!'

Jackson unwrapped the newspaper and found a mug with a small football on it and the Brazilian flag.

'You Brits love your footie, right?' said the Australian. 'And Brazil are the best.'

'Yeah, great!' said Jackson. A Brazil mug for an England supporter. It was a nice thought, sort of.

'Was your yacht any quicker?' asked Brooke.

'Abso-bloody-lutely! Your designs for the hull and the new hydrophobic sail material were great! I need to check the data, but I'd say she was givin' up heaps more speed.'

'Well, that's great,' said J.P. 'I'm hoping the same water-repellent nano-coating will work for *Verne*. I was just explaining to Brooke how important it is that our next underwater test is a successful one.' He cast a flinty stare at his daughter.

Brooke glared defiantly back at J.P. as he ushered Goulman away. She turned to Jackson, fuming. 'Explain to me why I put up with that man!'

'Er, because he's your dad and, unlike most dads, he lets you build robots in his laboratory.' Jackson tried not to get too excited at the thought of his own dad arriving in only a couple of days. 'Besides, you shouldn't have messed with that guy's car and you know it.'

They looked at each other and burst out laughing.

CHAPTER 5

The barbed fence was never going to hold back a hungry rainforest.

The soil in this part of Brazil was so thin and saturated with water that the roots of the trees around the Guillet Diamond Mine had risen up and become part of the perimeter.

Things grew so quickly here that the men guarding the entrance to the mining compound carried machetes – as well as machine guns, grenades and side arms. Hacking away the vines and roots that threatened to prevent the front gate from opening was a daily chore.

Inside the compound, in the middle of the night, a group of hardened and tired-looking men were loading wooden boxes on to a small flatbed lorry.

They had a uniform of sorts. All five of them wore flip-flops and jeans they'd cut off at the knees. Automatic weapons dangled on straps in front of T-shirts sporting phrases like CHILLAX and SKATE MONKEY.

One guard was chatting while he watched the other

four loading wooden crates on to the truck, when an arm appeared round his neck and a machete blade at his throat.

'Do you get paid to talk?' whispered a deep, crackly voice in Spanish.

'No, sir,' said the guard, his voice quivering.

'Correct. You get paid to guard. Now, either shut your mouth and do what I pay you for, or talk to my blade.'

'Yes, Boss!' said the guard, looking at his own petrified reflection in the polished steel in front of his face.

The blade belonged to Señor Guppy, the longest-serving head of security for the mine, an accolade earned by the fact that all previous security heads had died within a year of taking on the job. The mine had been attacked twelve times in its ten-year history, thirteen if you included the revolution, which had started with mining staff themselves and spread to the surrounding countryside.

Guppy's team had already fought off two raids and he was convinced that the only reason his forty-year-old body wasn't currently nourishing rainforest roots was because he was forever vigilant.

Guppy and two of his men joined the cargo in the back of the truck, then signalled to the two guards in the driver's cabin to move the vehicle out of the compound. As the gates swung open, two more guards on motocross bikes formed up in convoy, one in front and one behind the lorry.

The rainforest was at its most beautiful at night.

Guppy looked up. With the trees stretching straight up either side of the firebreak along which the convoy sped, he could clearly see a full moon.

Suddenly the engines on all three vehicles cut out, without warning, and Guppy jolted forward, knocking into the man next to him. The men on the truck started to talk, one of them calling to the outriders, until Guppy bellowed for them all to be quiet.

'Go on my command,' whispered Guppy to the two men beside him. 'I'll stay with the cargo.'

He cupped his hands and blew across his two thumbs forming the sound of a Great Horned Owl. The men in the cabin and on the motorcycles knew the sign.

The six guards fanned out around the truck in rehearsed formation, each man taking cover in the thick wall of trees and vegetation that surrounded them. No sooner had they assumed position than each of them became aware of the faint sound of air rushing all around them.

Guppy heard the first man scream and assumed one of his men had been knifed. He could see no sign of the man through the sights of his Steyr AUG assault rifle, but just caught a glimpse of a second of his men stagger- ing from behind a tree, gripping his stomach before dropping to the ground and joining in the moans of pain. Soon he was followed by a third, until Guppy could no longer see any of his six comrades; he only heard them groaning all around him.

Guppy swept the treeline with his gun sight, but could see no sign at all of the attackers.

Then the lights appeared.

A multitude of small dim red lights, spinning in a wide circle, traced the circumference of the fallen guards. They began to close slowly in, towards the truck – and towards Guppy.

As the burning lights wailed around him, Guppy could think of only one thing: Christ the Redeemer, the thirty-metre statue overlooking the barrio in which he'd been born and brought up. Only God could save him from the devil's own flying banshees now.

Guppy let his rifle clatter to the floor of the truck and crossed himself, at which point he suddenly understood what all the groaning was about. An invisible wave of pressure hit him. It seemed to be coming from the mysterious ring of lights, but Guppy was in no mood to worry about how or why, as he was gripped by a terrible and overwhelming agony in his stomach.

Just when it felt like his insides might actually explode, Señor Guppy spontaneously defecated.

CHAPTER 6

Only a few lights spoiled the uniform black of the building that rose against the fading sky like a big cliff.

As Jackson approached the entrance to the building, he punched some numbers into his phone and a single light – the one for his room on the seventh floor – came on.

In his first week on campus, Simmons Hall, the enormous dormitory building in which Jackson lived, had been the subject of an MIT hack. Among the university's students, famous examples of this tradition of large-scale practical jokes, or hacks, included a lifesize replica police car being placed on top of the Great Dome, the addition of two letters to the large chrome MIT sign so it read VOMIT, and glass boxes with chainsaws in them that appeared in lobbies with IN CASE OF ZOMBIE ATTACK! written on them.

For the Simmons Hall hack, a first-year electronics student had written a software program that could control the building's lighting from a web browser. One evening, he had made every light in all three hundred rooms flash simultaneously, turning the building into a giant lighthouse. Jackson, who by chance had met the boy the following day, had quietly suggested that by sequencing the lights mathematically they could be used to create a giant game of *Tetris*. The boy had given Jackson the codes to this secret server and the hack had been planned for the end of term. Jackson had finished the grid calculations for the building-sized computer game a few weeks ago; he just couldn't resist testing the system.

When he opened the door to his room, Jackson wished the phone's application extended to tidying up. If it weren't for the fact his dad was arriving tomorrow, he wouldn't have given the randomly distributed pants and socks on the floor a second glance.

Tomorrow would be the first time Jackson had seen his father in almost a year. They kept in regular contact; not as regular as Jackson would like, but then his father was resistant to anything he deemed more complicated than email and their weekly phone call.

As he tidied, he thought about his dad's words the last time they had spoken: *There's something I want to talk to you about.* It all sounded a bit ominous, but his dad had told him not to worry. It was probably nothing.

He began unpacking Goulman's mug from his bag. The newspaper wrapping fell to the floor and Jackson sighed – more stuff to clear up! But, as he bent down to pick it up, something caught his eye. It was a picture of two military guards curled up on what looked like a jungle floor, holding their stomachs in obvious pain. The tagline below the picture read: GAS ATTACK!

Jackson flattened out the newspaper page on his desk. The picture accompanied an article about a diamond robbery.

> Police are investigating a diamond heist, which took place near one of Brazil's largest diamond mines. The precious stones, which were in transit from the Guillet Diamond Mine, were intercepted by what local police suspect was a small mercenary force.
>
> Police Commissioner Enrico Sanchez said that he believes everyone in the armoured convoy transporting the stones had been gassed. 'The men were in a terrible state. All seven men had defecated and discharged so much bodily fluid that two of them were critically dehydrated and needed urgent hospital attention. We are looking at the possibility that the men were attacked using some form of gas or chemical.'

Sir Barry Scott, Security Director for the London-based company that owns the diamond mine, said that the haul of plain white diamonds, estimated at a value of around one hundred million dollars, was untraceable. 'These diamonds were raw and unprocessed. If they are cut, or subjected to the various colouring processes the industry uses to enhance raw stones, our investigators will have no way of identifying them once they pop up on the market.'

For a moment, Jackson froze. The picture of the men holding their stomachs and the description of their reaction to the 'gas' were very familiar to him. The MeX$_1$ dot. robots which Jackson and the other recruits had flown on missions for Lear had carried something called a Bass Bomb. The device – more like a very sophisticated speaker than a bomb – had caused exactly the same reaction in its victims. Its short blast of low-frequency sound didn't permanently damage a target, but caused them to lose control of their bowels in incredible pain.

But Lear was dead – MeX had been disgraced and closed down.

Jackson shook his head. The notion that the robbery

could have been carried out by MeX robots was preposterous. He needed to get over this sense of paranoia. For a good few months after Lear's disappearance, Jackson had seen connections to the maniacal billionaire and his rogue robots everywhere he looked. In his mind, every blacked-out 4x4 he spotted held MeX mercenaries waiting to fling the doors open and drag him inside. If ever someone he didn't know walked behind him on his way from school for more than a few minutes, he had them down for a kidnapper. And he'd pored over the newspaper and Internet accounts of Lear's disappearance, finding it hard to obtain the kind of irrefutable evidence of the man's death that he craved. For several weeks, he had become so paranoid he didn't leave the flat at all.

The MIT scholarship had been the chance for a clean start. Since moving to America, and getting wrapped up in the heavy load of college and lab work, Jackson had slowly got his head back together.

You're way too busy to be worrying about ghosts, he told himself, scrunching the newspaper page into a tight ball and throwing it in the bin. *Lear is dead.*

CHAPTER 7

Jackson's dad had one holiday outfit, regardless of where he was going – pressed white short-sleeved shirt, white nylon football shorts, black socks and trainers. His legs were so pale they were almost luminous.

Jackson waved vigorously as his father made his way through the crowd at airport arrivals, and greeted him with a big hug. He hadn't realized quite how much he'd missed him.

Mr Farley reciprocated with an awkward one-armed hug. 'You been waiting long, son?' he asked formally.

'Long enough.' Jackson had actually arrived an hour and a half early in his excitement to see his dad. 'You got any other bags?'

'Nope. This is me,' said Mr Farley, holding up a small cracked faux-leather kit bag. It was so old, Jackson was sure he remembered seeing it in photographs of his dad when *he* was a boy.

It wasn't a warm day, but Mr Farley insisted that the windows in the cab be left rolled down as they made their way to Cambridge, Massachusetts. 'Eight hours breathing other people's air,' he announced, before apologizing for his post-flight grumpiness. 'So this is Boston?' he said, staring out of the window as the taxi tracked alongside the Charles River. 'I still can't believe you're studying here.' He looked across at Jackson. 'Your mother would have been proud of you.'

After that, the job of keeping the conversation going was left to Jackson. He was used to this; his dad had always been a better listener than he was a talker. Jackson filled the brief journey time by recounting everything he knew about the approaching Boston skyline and the buildings of the university.

'Ever wondered what the front door of a nuclear reactor looks like?' asked Jackson as they cruised past the Fire Proof building. He pointed to what he knew looked like any old warehouse door.

'Your university has its own nuclear reactor?' his dad asked, slightly horrified.

'Sure. MIT is one of a handful of colleges in the world that trains the nuclear physicists of the future!' said Jackson. He imagined himself introducing his dad to the wonders of Cambridge and MIT and enjoying the look of amazement on his face.

The cab crossed an intersection and pulled up at a modern-looking hotel. Jackson waited while his dad checked in and then the two of them walked the short distance back to the Fire Proof building. Jackson led his father down to the basement level and they entered the vast laboratory. His dad stopped in his tracks, clearly amazed.

'Cool, huh?' said Jackson nonchalantly, but secretly pleased with his dad's reaction to the huge laboratory.

Mr Farley gazed around the room, his eyes tracing the long line of scientific apparatus that stretched along the back wall and then stopping at the elevator cage containing *Tin Lizzie*.

'That's a Hummer, right? Like the American army use?' Jackson's dad asked, pointing at Brooke's car.

'Yes and no. It's a Hummer H3R, the civilian version of what the military use. It belongs to Brooke. It's self-driving, Dad.'

'It drives itself? Really? Isn't that dangerous?'

Jackson laughed. His father had in fact, unknowingly, once seen *Tin Lizzie* in action. It was via a remote link on Jackson's bedroom computer monitor – Jackson had linked to the car and driven it remotely in an attempt to rescue Brooke from a hideaway in the mountains of Arizona. He recalled how his dad had made him switch off what he took for a 'driving game'. It was an act that almost led to the two-tonne off-roader flying off a cliff with Brooke still in it.

There was a lot that Jackson had never been able to tell his father. It was the thing he hated most about his double life – having to hide his involvement with MeX and then make up excuses for the fact he'd become a virtual recluse after the information that he and Brooke gave had led to the downfall of the organization. It was hard to lead a normal existence when you feared for your life. He'd told his dad he was feeling a little down, which was their code for the times when they missed Jackson's mum. But even that didn't wash after a couple of months. His dad had tried to talk to him, which Jackson knew had been difficult for someone so uncomfortable with expressing feelings, but even then Jackson could never have told him the real truth.

Jackson looked at his dad. He was gingerly fingering a large piece of wispy transparent film, slung between a desk and the wall.

'It's just a hammock. Feel free to climb in,' said Jackson.

'But it's made of cling film, isn't it? Won't it just rip?'

'It's a super-strong cling wrap, made of a nano-engineered compound which emulates the organic thread of a spider. You'll be fine; that section alone is strong enough to support the weight of a car.'

Farley Senior shook his head in disbelief. 'Astonishing. But I'll give it a miss if it's all the same.'

'You might like to see these,' said Jackson, indicating the section of the laboratory reserved for the robots. If there was one part of his and Brooke's work at MIT that Jackson most wanted his dad to see, it was the robots. Both Jackson and Brooke had a passion for designing, building and programming all manner of robotic machines – Brooke for the potential of how they could help people, and Jackson for the love and utter fascination of the science involved. Jackson knew his move to America had been hard on his dad. He hoped the line-up of robots might help his dad to realize it was all worthwhile.

Jackson walked along the robot line-up. 'Say hello to *Punk*, *Verne*, *Fist*, *Tug* and *Tread*.'

Each machine was in its designated pen, the aluminium structures built to support them so they could be charged and worked on from several angles.

'I like the look of the yellow one. *Fist*, was it? What's he do?'

'A bit of everything really. The clue's in his name: Fire, Industry, Security, Tactical. He's based around a combination of memory metal and hydrogen fuel-cell technology.'

'Memory metal?'

'Strands of steel filament, which tighten when an electrical current is passed through them and then relax when it's turned off. *Fist* is made up of four separate robotic hands that when combined, are as powerful as a car crusher.'

'But its hands can only be three times bigger than mine. How can they produce that amount of pressure?'

'You want the technical answer?' asked Jackson, relishing the opportunity to impress his dad with his knowledge.

'Try me.'

'Quantum mechanical and electrostatic effects present on the nanoscale,' said Jackson.

Mr Farley's eyes widened. *Good*, thought Jackson, *he's impressed*.

'And what are they . . . remote control?' asked Mr Farley.

'We call them dot.robots – because they're remotely controlled via the Internet. And this is what we use to control them!' Jackson pulled his mobile phone from his pocket.

'If the robot I'm controlling can see – like *Punk*, *Tread* or *Verne* – I can feed the video stream from their cameras to the handset or any other connected device.'

Jackson held the phone up so his father could see it. Lacking any buttons or even a hint of a screen, it looked, to all intents and purposes, like a thin, shiny, white plastic slab.

Jackson handed the phone to his dad who flipped it over in his hands a few times before looking up and shrugging his shoulders in bewilderment.

'Touch where you think the screen should be,' suggested Jackson.

His dad did as instructed and the whole surface of the phone transformed into a full-colour screen, showing a virtual desktop and various icons.

'The plastic contains microscopic phosphorescent

particles – front and back, the whole phone is one big display.

Jackson's dad shook his head in disbelief.

'And you'll love this . . .' Jackson walked over to Brooke's desk and grabbed another identical-looking handset. He held them both up in front of his dad and they clipped together, magnetically, end to end. Immediately the colour screen extended across the second phone, forming one long widescreen display on the surface of both devices.

Jackson pulled the phones apart again, placing one of the handsets on the desk and keeping the other in his hand.

'One phone is all I need to operate any of the dot. robots in this lab. I can control them by touching virtual controls on the phone's surface or by simply drawing gestures in the air!'

'And you worked on all these things?' asked Mr Farley.

'Yes, Dad. I worked up the numbers. I do the maths for all of Brooke's projects. Here's something she's working on right now.'

Jackson motioned to a pile of carbon fibre and titanium components on a desk. 'Brooke calls it her portable robot Chauffeur. It's a miniaturized version of the robotics that automate *Tin Lizzie*. They are small enough to be stored in a holdall. The kit of parts can be retro-fitted to just about any four-wheeled vehicle to make it self-driving.'

'Jackson, this is incredible work you're doing. Really. But I hope you're also doing your schoolwork. To leave this place with a degree, at your age . . . you could pick any job you wanted. And name your price!'

Jackson didn't mind the gentle rebuke. It was really important to him that his dad understood and appreciated the work he and Brooke did – even though his praise, as was his dad's way, came with a piece of practical advice attached.

'It's college work, not schoolwork, Dad, and everything I do here counts towards it. I only have to attend a couple of lectures a week to cover my degree. The mathematical theory I can do with my eyes shut. Generally, it's stuff I've already read up on – infinite-dimensional algebra, probability theory . . . one of my lecturers even turned up dressed as Darth Vader! He did the whole hour on quantum cosmology without taking his mask off!'

Jackson could see from the change in his dad's expression that he wasn't too keen on much more detail – he'd just wanted to know his son was meeting his academic obligations. Jackson changed tack.'What d'you say we get something to eat? You must be bushed after the flight.'

They ate at the hotel, which Jackson was impressed to find had some of MIT's most famous mathematical equations for wallpaper and patent applications for pictures. Jackson couldn't be sure, but as they sat in the hotel restaurant, he thought his father seemed more distant than usual, and he had to work doubly hard to keep the one-sided conversation going. Jackson put it down to jet lag and his dad's need to catch up on sleep.

But the next morning when Jackson met his dad at the hotel to do a tour of Cambridge, it didn't seem like much had changed. His dad was so quiet that Jackson couldn't remember a time when he'd had to talk so much. His self-styled urban safari took in his favourite book-shops, some of MIT's kookier buildings like Simmons Hall, the dorm building opposite his own which he thought looked like a giant space invader, and the higgledy-piggledy Stata Center, a collection of crooked, metal-clad towers that looked like they should buckle and fall at any minute. They walked through endless corridors and giant lecture theatres and laboratories, and roamed the labyrinthine service tunnels that snaked underneath the campus and dated back to before the Second World War.

But none of Jackson's campus tour elicited any more than nods and token questions. Jackson's jet-lag theory began to look shaky and he wondered if his dad had something on his mind he wasn't telling him.

Finally, they arrived at the top of some wide stone steps leading to Gillian Court, the name given to the wide lawn below the university's Great Dome. 'And when I want space to think,' said Jackson pointedly, looking at his dad, 'I come here.'

Mr Farley looked at the beautiful lawn as shards of golden sunlight cut through a thick canopy of garish purple clouds and formed perfect geometric shapes on it. Rain was a certainty.

The two of them sat at the top of the steps, as Jackson often did, gazing out over the lawn before the inevitable downpour came. Jackson and his dad always did silence well; it was part of what it took for them to live together. All the same, Jackson was now convinced there was something about this particular lack of conversation that wasn't right. Even after nine months apart, he was aware of a tension between himself and his father, not unlike the pressure of the gathering storm.

'Is everything OK, Dad?' he asked.

It was as if the question was an injection of something Mr Farley needed to wake him up. He got to his feet, took a couple of thoughtful paces, and then turned back to Jackson.

'I have something important to talk to you about,' he said. 'Your mother and I have kept something from you, Jackson. We agreed to tell you on your twelfth birthday, but it's been such an extraordinary year and what with you getting ready to come here and everything . . . I couldn't find the right time.'

'Just tell me,' Jackson said, trying to help his dad who, for some reason, was obviously struggling.

'Jackson,' he said, his body now still, but his voice unsteady. 'I am not your biological father.'

Jackson couldn't speak.

His dad looked unsure what to do next and so carried on, his voice wavering as he spoke. 'When your mum and I first met, she already had you. You were just over a year old. We discussed telling you so many times, Jackson, but we were afraid it might change things between us. But it shouldn't change things.' He bent down towards Jackson. 'That is . . . I'm still your dad!'

But Jackson could only sit frozen on the stone step, stunned. 'You're not, though, are you?' he said. 'And if you're not my real father, then who is?'

His dad visibly flinched. 'That's just it, Jackson, I don't know. Your mother refused to tell me. She insisted it was between you and her.'

'But she's dead!' Jackson was surprised how angrily he'd fired the words out. 'You can't tell me something like that and just leave me hanging!'

'I'm sorry. She wouldn't tell me. What could I do, son?'

Son. The word seemed to hang in the air.

Jackson couldn't help it; his emotions suddenly became a combustible mix. 'You could have insisted she told you!' he yelled. 'You could have made her tell you.'

'You know Mum.' Mr Farley tried a gentle smile.

'What chance did I have of changing her mind, son?'

'Stop calling me that!' Jackson intended the comment as a slap.

The noxious mixture of anger and hurt continued to bubble away, making Jackson feel hot. Even the rain, which was now sweeping in across the lawn and dancing up the steps, couldn't cool him down.

'I wish you'd hadn't come here. I've been fine without you!' he said, turning and storming towards the Great Dome.

'Jackson, wait! We need to talk about this!'

But Jackson had already disappeared inside the building.

CHAPTER 8

Jackson saw his dad once more before he left for London. It was at the airport departure gate. Brooke had frog-marched him there. His dad hugged him, but Jackson didn't hug him back. His dad also gave him his birthday present. Jackson put the small parcel in his coat pocket, where it had stayed ever since.

That was five days ago. Jackson had hardly left his dorm since, surfacing to buy pizza and chocolate then returning to his room. He'd managed to avoid everyone's attempts to contact him, including Brooke's, which came in the form of hourly text messages. She'd even sat outside his dorm room just talking, before he told her he was fine and to leave him alone. Jackson just couldn't seem to clear his head. All he could do was read. Books were good for numbing the pain. He wasn't particularly bothered what he read, but facts were good – advanced number theory, statistics, a thick textbook he'd borrowed from J.P. called *Artificial Intelligence* – they were good antidotes, some reality.

It was J.P.'s book that indirectly led to Jackson eventually leaving his pit of a room. The author, a retired robotics expert called Professor Singer, was giving a lecture on campus. Since he was reading the book, Jackson thought he might as well see what the professor had to say.

'Singer is an oddball,' J.P. had said when he handed Jackson the book. 'But he's also a genius! He's been designing computerized brains since before I was in diapers.'

The lecture hall was like the auditorium of a theatre. Rows of seating formed a crescent in front of a large stage where a small man in a white lab coat sat behind a desk, reading. Beside him stood something, roughly a metre and a half high, mysteriously draped in a black cloth.

Jackson glanced at the other students as they filed in and took a seat. His experience of student life at MIT was nothing like his school life in Peckham. The students here, most of them five or six years his senior, were some of the world's most exceptionally gifted young people. They came from all over the world – India, China, Australia and, of course, the USA – and they were rarely, if ever, late. Unlike his fellow pupils back in Peckham, they didn't chat during lectures or ask questions designed to undermine the teacher. And, based on the complexity of the answers they gave when prompted, they had always read up on the subject they'd come to hear about.

As part of his arrangement with J.P., Jackson was required to attend several lectures to qualify for his MIT degree. The rest of his course was taken care of by the work he did with Brooke's robots. So far he had attended a bunch of lectures on: number theory, which he loved because they included his favourite topic, prime numbers; three classes on quantum cryptography, which covered the making and breaking of secret codes; and a couple of advanced probability theory lectures – Jackson loved these because they suggested it was possible to predict the outcome of things in the future, using just the power of maths.

Shame the theory didn't stretch to predicting who his real father might be, Jackson thought. But before he could sink back into depression over his parentage, Jackson's train of thought was interrupted abruptly by Professor Singer suddenly throwing down his book and striding to the front of the stage.

'Robots are going to take over the world!' he declared. Smiles and raised eyebrows appeared on many of the faces in the audience at this opening statement. The professor carried on. 'But not until they learn to think better! Thinking robots are, of course, already a part of most of our lives. This robot is a thinker,' he said, patting the covered object.

Jackson looked at the object. Its outline was a little robot-like – a small rectangular head atop a large boxy body.

The professor stooped over a laptop on his desk and pressed a few keys. Several lines of numbers and symbols, which made up the computer code, streamed down the centre of a large projector screen behind him. 'And here's the code for my thinking robot – see if you can work out what kind of robot it is, before I reveal it!'

A good proportion of the room leaned forward and squinted at the code, trying to decipher it.

'Any ideas?' asked the professor.

'Some kind of unmanned military vehicle?' said a guy on the front row confidently.

'Why do you say that?' asked the professor.

'Well, if that's just a box under that cover, it looks about the right size to contain a UAV. And that code seems to be encrypted.'

The professor smiled. 'Anyone else?'

'A surgery robot?' suggested a girl who was sitting a few rows in front of Jackson.

'Interesting,' the professor observed.

He ambled over to the object. 'Say hello to Soapy, everyone!' And with a flourish, he pulled the black material away.

Jackson was surprised to see a washing machine, with a box of washing detergent on top of it.

The room erupted into laughter.

J.P. was right, thought Jackson. *He is an oddball.*

'The humble washing machine answers most common

definitions of what a robot is: it has sensors; it has a brain; it can do the work of a man or a woman; it can move. At least mine can . . . all around the kitchen when it's on full spin!' More polite laughter. 'But can it think? Well, sort of. The standard code of this machine, straight out of the factory, which is what you can see behind me, is designed to help the robot perform some simple reactive behaviours – like check that you've added washing powder or that it's not overheating.'

The professor punched another key and a new batch of code loaded on the screen. This time it began to scroll down and continued as Professor Singer carried on speaking.

'But this new AI code, which has taken me and my MIT team over a year to write, has taken Soapy to the next level. Now, rather than reacting to stimuli with stodgy, predetermined responses, Soapy can apply his own logic. He can think for himself.'

The professor walked to his desk and typed a sentence into his laptop, which came up on the screen.

`Hello, Soapy.`

After a few seconds a text reply materialized on the screen:

`Hi there!`

'Soapy's AI program is available on the MIT Intranet along with other artificial intelligence codes – and I'm happy for those of you taking this module to download and play with it.'

Everyone except Jackson applauded. It was impressive, but he wasn't in the mood to celebrate. Jackson's attention began to drift elsewhere. The robotics of a washing machine weren't enough to keep him sufficiently distracted. He gazed around the auditorium and found himself wondering if anyone else here didn't know their father.

A dark cloud hung over him. His dad's visit had left him with so many unanswered questions. What did his real dad look like? Did he even know he had a son? Was he still alive?

Jackson fired up the browser on his mobile phone and entered his mum's name into the search window. Perhaps there might be some answers among the thousands of algorithmically indexed search results.

Tens of Bernice Margaret Farleys covered one side of the plastic phone. He was able to spot the irrelevant ones almost immediately: his mother had never been on Facebook and she certainly wasn't chairlady of the Kentucky Women's Medieval Reenactment Society.

He fingered through page after page of nonsensical links by touching his phone's surface, and was about to give up when a headline caught his eye. It was a link to the 'Death Notices' section of the *Peckham News*. Jackson knew the newspaper, which was delivered free to hundreds of homes in his area. The link featured the words 'In remembrance of Bernice Farley of Peckham'.

He had seen this before. His dad kept a copy of it in a red box-file in their sitting room, along with other Mum-related memorabilia, like her diaries and letters his parents had written to each other.

Jackson had looked in the box once or twice, but he'd never been able to bring himself to read his mother's obituary.

He took a deep breath and clicked on the link.

Bernice Farley of Peckham, south-east London, 38, died Saturday 16 June, in St Thomas's Hospital where she was taken after a hit and run accident. Services will be Friday at 10 a.m. at Sacred Heart Church with Pastor Delroy Croyde officiating.

Mrs Farley, whose maiden name was Lloyd, was born in Lewisham, London. She graduated from Oxford with a Masters Degree before marrying Mr James Farley.

She is survived by her husband and son, Jackson Farley.

Jackson had a hollow feeling in the pit of his stomach like he always did when something took him back to his mother's accident, but he tried his best to ignore it; there was too much in front of him that he was curious about. His mother's maiden name for starters – it hadn't occurred to him to use that. Now it was in front of him, it seemed so obvious. What he needed to be searching for was information about his mother's life before she met his dad – before she was a Farley.

Jackson entered 'Bernice Lloyd' into Google. There were several references to Bernice Lloyd on various social networks, but little that looked like it related to his mum.

Jackson flipped his handset over in his hand, so the phone's all-over screen showed previously viewed pages in a series of small boxes. He touched a small square and the obituary enlarged. His attention was drawn to the mention of Oxford University. His mum had often talked to him about her student days reading Applied Mathematics at Jesus College. He tried another search: Bernice Lloyd + Oxford University. This time the third entry down offered up something that jarred his memory: 'Oxford University's official Alumni remember maths team members past and present.'

The link revealed a page with a royal blue insignia at the top of it and the words UNIVERSITY OF OXFORD MATHS TEAMS emblazoned below it.

There was a picture, featuring a group of four geeky-looking students, which Jackson took to be the current maths team. To its left was an arrow leading to the maths teams of previous years. Jackson wasn't entirely sure when his mother had attended the university, but he certainly remembered her talking about being on the Oxford maths team.

By continually clicking the arrow, he was able to move, in reverse chronological order, through a slideshow of maths team members.

After several pages filled with the proud faces of mostly bespectacled brainboxes, he eventually came across a page that was slightly different from the others; it featured the year of the team and, on a gold rosette, the words WINNERS OF THE SPECIAL MATHS OLYMPIAD. Above the rosette, in between her fellow teammates, Jackson spotted his mum. It was a younger face than he remembered and the kind of big hair he'd have never let her forget if he'd been given the chance, but that broad, warm smile was unmistakable.

His mum had talked with pride about how her team had been the first group of Oxford students for several years to win the coveted Mathematics Olympiad. She'd even kept the competition questions. Jackson remembered he had struggled with the transformational geometry part of the question paper and that his mother was quicker, initially, at the workings out for Fermat's and Euler's theorems, but by his seventh birthday he could finish the paper in half the time it took his mum.

Jackson shot a quick glance down at the stage as he

sensed a shift in the audience's attention. Flanked by the projector screen, Professor Singer was talking about teaming up different types of intelligent robots to help each other complete tasks. Beside him on the projector screen were two cartoon drawings of washing machines – one with a smiling face and one with a sad face. Above them it read: COMPLEMENTARY PERSONALITIES: HOW TO MAKE MACHINES WORK TOGETHER.

Jackson's attention was caught.

'As some of you may know, for many years I have run a famous final-term AI competition.' The professor looked intently at the audience of students. 'This year I'd like entrants to experiment with some of my ideas about complementary personalities. I want to know how you would team up different types of intelligent robots so that each might help the other complete tasks. There's no prize, just the prestige associated with winning. But I will allow the winner to let Soapy do a load of their washing – I know how grubby you students are!' There was a ripple of laughter from the auditorium. 'You can use any of the AI code I've uploaded as a starting point. You have two weeks to email me a copy of your finished code.'

It was definitely an interesting thought, but Jackson had bigger things on his mind right now. When Singer moved on to his next subject, Jackson looked back down at his handset.

Peering closely at his mum's photograph, he examined

the faces of the other three students who stood beside his mother in the photograph. Below each was a name: B. Lloyd for his mum, then Lumpy, D. Alexander and Mr Pope.

Jackson looked more carefully at the three young men who stood in a huddle around his mother. Lumpy was a squat man with a thick ginger beard and an implausibly large and scruffy jumper that reached his knees. Next to him was D. Alexander, a tall, scrawny young man whose most distinguishing feature was the smoker's pipe between his teeth – it was the kind of curly black pipe you might expect an old fisherman to have, rather than a university student in his early twenties. And the third team member wore a baseball cap with large dark sunglasses, which did nothing to hide a profusion of red spots on his face that they were obviously intended to disguise.

Jackson shook his head in frustration as he realized he'd been examining each of the maths team members for fatherhood potential, mentally ticking them off based on features such as the ginger gene and bad acne.

This is ridiculous, he told himself. *I'm auditioning dads!*

He switched off the browser of his phone and looked up to see the professor in mid-flow. The lecture had moved on and the screen behind the professor now read SWARM AND MODULAR ROBOTICS. Below the headline were some more cartoon-like illustrations of tiny cube-shaped machines joined up in different formations – a snake, a square and a ring.

'The reconfiguration of various modules enables the modular robot to assume almost any shape imaginable.' Professor Singer walked up and down in front of the screen. 'While in distinctly different categories of robotics, robotic swarms and modular robot designs both get their strength from their numbers. For the swarm, it's about large numbers of small simple machines working together and sharing a single insect-like swarm intelligence in order to perform tasks they couldn't do individually.'

Jackson had read about these kinds of robots in Professor Singer's book and found it really interesting.

'Several large corporations have been developing swarm and modular robot technology.' A slide appeared behind the professor containing some company logos and he talked briefly about each company's robot projects. Jackson took notes until the professor said something that caused him to drop his pen with a clatter on the floor. *Lear Corporation*, Devlin Lear's company.

Jackson scrabbled down by his feet for his pen, completely flustered now. He looked at the slide again, staring intently at each of the logos on the screen. He should have looked properly the first time. One of them really was Devlin Lear's corporation logo.

The professor continued his summary of the company's history. 'Of course, following the tragic death of Lear, Lear Corp has been disbanded.'

Tragic death? thought Jackson. The only *tragedy*, as far as Jackson was concerned, was that Lear had got away with his criminal deeds and had affected the lives of so many innocent people before he'd drowned.

'The organization funded several projects aimed at advancing the design and testing of swarm and modular robotics. They were subjects Lear was extremely passionate about. The man really was a hero of modern computing and he'll be sorely missed.'

The professor was obviously completely blinded by Lear's scientific credentials and didn't appear to be concerned by the reports that the world had heard about his criminal past. Hearing Lear talked about in such respected terms sickened Jackson to the pit of his stomach. If, like Jackson, Brooke and the Kojima twins, the professor had been tricked by Lear into taking part in criminal acts that had led to at least one death that Jackson knew of, then Lear wouldn't seem heroic at all.

Disgusted, Jackson decided that coming to Singer's lecture hadn't been such a good idea after all.

Jackson rose to his feet and moved out towards the exit.

'Leaving so soon, young man?'

Jackson ignored the sarcastic address from the professor and walked out of the door – he had nothing to say to him.

*

The steps outside the lecture theatre led to a wide lawn with a soaring pine tree in the centre. Jackson let his gaze drift to the crest of the tree, silhouetted behind a sparkling sun. He breathed in deeply, the soothing concoction of fresh air and tranquillity allowing the frustrations of the lecture theatre to slowly ebb away.

As he walked across the grass, Jackson activated the email application on his phone – there was something he felt ready to do now. So he began to write.

Dear Dad,

I'm sorry for the way I reacted last week. I was really angry. I still am! But you kind of turned my entire life upside down with the whole 'I'm not your dad' speech! I was so angry I could have punched someone. I could have punched you! (I'm glad I didn't, by the way.)

I've been doing a lot of thinking since you left.

I think you should have told me before, but what I'm saying is that I forgive you – because I can see that having me to deal with after Mum died must have made it really hard – and because I know you'll be feeling rubbish right now.

Now DON'T GET ANNOYED but I want you to do something for me – in return for me not ignoring you for the rest of my life. I want to find out more about Mum. I miss her and I want to know as much about her as you do.

So, if I promise to give it back, could you send me that stash of her stuff you keep under the sofa?

Thanks, Dad.

C U soon,

Jackson x

PS If you see anyone from school, tell them to tell Mr Willard, my history teacher, that Boston is v. cool and that I think they've forgiven us for the whole Tea Party fiasco.

CHAPTER 9

The next morning Jackson felt a little better. Writing to his dad had helped him get some of the things he was feeling off his chest. It wasn't just about discovering more about his mum – and maybe even his real father. It was the feeling that without his dad, he didn't really have anyone any more. And, besides, he'd missed him.

Despite this, though, Jackson's heart was still heavy – after all, his mum had kept things from him too. And that hurt.

With these feelings and Professor Singer's lecture about Lear weighing heavy on his mind, Jackson had decided he needed to get out of his room and force himself to follow Atticus79 to chess club. He didn't really want to go, but he knew it was good for him.

As they walked from the dorm building to the lawn in the centre of campus where the chess club regularly met, Atticus79's virtually unbroken stream of consciousness about 'mineral properties' was proving the ideal antidote to Jackson's state of mind. The young geologist's passionate description of anthracite mining methods and the magnetic qualities of magnetite didn't leave much room for Jackson to ponder his own problems too deeply.

When they reached the chess club's meeting place, below MIT's Great Dome, Jackson noticed that several of the club members weren't there, but had joined a small crowd of students who were all staring up at the top of the building.

Jackson gazed up at the imposing dome and was amazed to see that its surface had been decorated with large conical spikes.

'It's a hack,' said Atticus79. 'It's very cool, but I'm not sure what it's supposed to be.'

'I know exactly what it is,' laughed Jackson for the first time in days. 'It's *Punk!*'

Jackson called Brooke and congratulated her on her very risky but extremely cool way of distracting him from everything that had been going on lately, and they made a date to meet at Jackson's favourite cafe.

There were three things about Cyber Republic that Jackson liked: you could buy proper English tea here ('builder's tea', as his dad called it), which meant milky, super-sweet tea strong enough for the spoon to stand up in. Jackson had tried to make the physics of that particular definition work, but he hadn't managed it yet. You could also use the free Wi-Fi and each table had its own power point, which dangled, like a chandelier, from the ceiling.

What he was less impressed by, however, was the amount of ice that arrived in the Coke he had ordered. It had always bugged him, and the big cardboard cup was so brimful of ice cubes when he picked it up from the counter that he wondered if there was any room left for his drink.

Finding a bench by the window, he looked out across the busy street. No sign of Brooke. It was exactly 12 p.m.

Jackson turned his attention to the problem of the ice cubes. He held the one-litre tub up to his mouth and attempted to guide a stream of Coke around the icy rock pile and into his mouth. Three mouthfuls later and it was all over. Too little liquid, too warm.

Jackson considered the problem. He'd paid for a one-litre cup of Coke and that's what he expected to get. What he'd been given was about eighty per cent pure ice, with Coke that was too warm if you drank it quickly, but too cold and diluted if you left it swishing around the iceberg.

Jackson considered the drinks he got out of his fridge back in his dorm to be the ideal temperature. The dial inside his fridge was set to $1.5°C$, so he decided he'd aim for a Coke that was $1.5°$ Centigrade.

He grabbed a pen from his inside pocket and wrote a formula at the top of a napkin.

Ice melting + Ice going up to 1.5°C = Drink going down to 1.5°C

He then proceeded to cover the rest of the napkin in calculations, pausing only briefly to enter 'Energy required to turn ice to water?' into the search engine on his phone.

Finally, he noted that about seventy-five per cent of the ice in his cup had melted in the three minutes he'd been doing his sums. He added 0.75x to the top of the napkin and adjusted the rest of the workings out accordingly.

'Keeping yourself out of mischief I see!' It was Brooke.

'You're early,' said Jackson.

'I'm thirsty,' replied Brooke.

'What would you like?' Jackson asked, getting up.

'Well, that's what I call service,' Brooke replied. 'I'll have a lemonade, please.'

Jackson thought the guy at the counter had an uncanny resemblance to Gordon Freeman from the video game *Half Life* – dishevelled brown hair, large geeky black spectacles and a perfectly trimmed goatee.

'A lemonade, please,' said Jackson.

'Sure thing, man,' said Gordon.

'But this time I'd like exactly 840.3 millilitres of liquid.'

'You would?' said the real-life video-game character, at a loss.

'Yeah! And 10.6 ice cubes. Please.'

'Point six – you say?'

'Uh huh!'

'Any particular reason for that?'

Jackson slipped the napkin on to the counter.

Ice melting + Ice going up to 1.5°C = Drink going down to 1.5°C

$$0.75x \times 333 + 0.69x \times 4.2 \times 1.5 = (1000 - 0.92x)\, 4.2 \times 12.5$$

$$249.75x + 4.347x = 52500 - 48.3x$$

$$302.397x = 52500$$

Amount of ice x ¡ 173.6 g

Amount of drink $1000 - 0.92 \times 173.6 = 840.3$ ml

Total ice cubes $\underline{173.6} = 10.6$ ice cubes

Gordon glanced at the arithmetical scribbles packed tightly on to the paper napkin, then looked back at Jackson with a resigned expression.

'Hey, whatever feeds your needs, dude.'

'There you are,' said Jackson, placing Brooke's drink in front of her. 'It will be at the optimum temperature in around two and half minutes' time.'

'Right,' said Brooke, smiling. 'Of course it will!' She knew Jackson well enough to be unfazed by his mathematical exactitude.

'So, come on, how did you get those spikes up there?' asked Jackson.

'A good magician never reveals her tricks.'

'I'm guessing *Fist* was involved?'

'What, let one of my robots out, without my father's consent?' said Brooke with a mischievous glint in her eye. 'Anyway, it doesn't matter how I did it; the important thing is that my little Batman beacon worked. *You* picked up and called me.'

Jackson tapped his fingers nervously on the table. He wasn't quite ready to tell Brooke everything that had happened in the last few days. 'How's your lemonade?' he said, changing the subject.

'It's fine. Look, you don't have to tell me what's going on between you and your dad. But you need to return my calls!'

'Yeah, I'm sorry about that.' Jackson felt bad. None of this was Brooke's fault. And not calling her wasn't helping. He was still angry and upset. He was no closer to finding out anything about his mum or real dad that might help him understand things better. Even so, the mere thought of opening up about how he felt to Brooke – or anyone for that matter – made him cringe. He looked up to find Brooke staring him straight in the face, waiting for an explanation.

'All right, I understand what you're saying. I'm just feeling homesick. I'm OK now.'

There was an awkward silence between the two of them, as Brooke decided whether or not to pursue the subject. They both knew Brooke wasn't buying it, but to Jackson's relief she decided to move on.

'I heard you stormed out of Singer's AI class yesterday?'

'Yes, well, you should have heard what he was saying about Lear. He called him a *hero*. It made my blood boil.'

'A lot of people didn't believe Lear was corrupt, despite the evidence we posted on the Net. I guess Singer is one of them.'

'He said his death was a tragedy. I wish I could have told him about that man we saw killed on the Ukraine mission.'

Brooke didn't say anything. She'd been deeply affected by what they had seen on their MeX mission last summer.

It was in a compound in Ukraine where they'd learned about Devlin Lear's evil plan to steal millions of litres of water and seen his heartless treatment of hundreds of homeless locals. More than a year on and Jackson still remembered the horrific things they'd witnessed there.

It was strange, but the two of them hadn't talked about Lear for a long time. Jackson had supposed that Brooke felt the same way he did – he just wanted to move on. He'd spent the best part of the last twelve months learning to stop looking over his shoulder. Brooke, who'd been kidnapped by Lear, must have felt it even more. She was unusually quiet now.

'Anyway, Singer obviously doesn't know what he's

talking about with regards to that man.' Jackson was worried he'd upset Brooke by bringing it up, but she smiled at Jackson's attempt to bring her back from her thoughts.

'True. No one does except for us. But Dad says the professor has some quite brilliant things to say about robotics. Did you stay long enough to hear any of it?'

'Very funny. The stuff about swarm robotics is interesting,' said Jackson.

'Ah, yes! The idea of small robots working together to make one big one has been around for a while. Goulman and J.P. did some work on that technology last year – it's actually where the electromagnetic coupling that enables our phones to stick together, and share a screen, comes from. The two of them got a few basic modular robots to find each other and form shapes, but then Dad got the government contract for *Verne* and put Goulman on it instead. I remember, they fell out about that. You see, I'm not the only one who finds Dad hard to work with!'

'Now you mention it, the professor did have some interesting things to say about complementary personalities.'

'What, like you and me, you mean?' said Brooke, trying to get a smile out of him.

'Smart and bossy? Yes, I guess – that works.' Jackson grinned. 'He's running a competition. It made me wonder about *Tug* and *Punk*. You never know, Brooke, it could be your best chance ever of actually winning something!'

'Now don't get smart!' said Brooke, proceeding to nois-ily suck the final dregs of lemonade through a straw. 'What about the fact that they're top secret? I'm already in so much trouble for our latest stunt with *Fist*.'

'He just wants to see the code. I can easily hide their identity. More importantly, we can run the code for real – we could actually give them brains!'

'Give a spiked wrecking ball and a flying battering ram the ability to think and act on their own?' said Brooke.

Jackson could see the idea had got the cogs inside Brooke's engineer's head turning. 'Precisely.'

'And might a project like this stop you moping around your dorm room?'

'I think it would,' said Jackson.

'Then let's do it!'

'Really?'

'Don't be so surprised.' Brooke grinned. 'After all, we do have complementary personalities!'

CHAPTER 10

Over the next few days Jackson and Brooke transformed the laboratory into something that resembled an operating theatre.

Carrying out the ideas they had picked up from Professor Singer was a complex procedure, but it helped that *Punk* and *Tug* already had the required hardware. They each had a bank of sixteen multi-core processors. These 'brains' decided everything from how to navigate to which battery to draw power from when a surge of energy was required to move faster or electrocute an unfortunate target. The robots also possessed some Artificial Intelligence already in the shape of their fly-by-wire flight management systems.

Since the dawn of the computer age, thanks to the ability of computers to perform lightning quick calculations, processors had been used to keep even the most unwieldy of machines airborne – the F16 Fighting Falcon, the Eurofighter and the Stealth Bomber were all examples of aircraft that needed more than a pilot's brain to stay in the air. With computers constantly monitoring and micro-adjusting every flap and surface, it was theoretically possible to make a dining-room chair fly. Brooke had built the same kind of technology into *Punk* and *Tug* – thousands of lines of code and assorted hardware modules kept them in the air, while their remote operators, Brooke and Jackson, simply pointed them in the direction they wanted them to fly.

Brooke and Jackson had spent the last two days working at providing their robots with the ability to join the dots – the ability to think entirely for themselves and link what they already knew about flying, navigating and scanning to a series of simple tasks. Using GPS, for example, *Punk* could already work out the quickest route between waypoints, or markers on a map. He had a focused beam of infrared radiation, which enabled him to see targets in the dark or people lost in the thick smoke of a burning building. And he had radio detection and ranging, or radar, which could magically highlight terrain and objects miles in the distance by bouncing pulses of high-frequency electromagnetic waves off them. But the key point was that at the moment neither *Punk* nor *Tug* could act on any of this information independently of whoever was controlling them – they just couldn't join the dots.

Importantly, there were two subtle differences in the way Jackson was coding the two robots. *Tug* was designed to be the daredevil of the duo, fearless and forceful in the face of a challenge, whereas *Punk*'s new AI programming was designed to make him more cautious and analytical – two contrasting personalities, designed to complement each other and provide the best possible chance of completing a task successfully.

Brooke couldn't help but notice that her plan to drag Jackson out of his doldrums, by focusing him on a project, was working. She might not be any closer to knowing what had gone on during his father's visit, but in contrast to the last few days he was feverish with enthusiasm. None of the problems they came against could curb his energy for the project, as he excitedly programmed and scrawled numbers and mathematical symbols on every available surface, including the glass doors of J.P.'s office.

At around 1 p.m. on the third day, Jackson surfaced from a particularly intense typing session in which he'd worked out the final code sequences he needed.

'OK, that should do it,' he said, popping up from under the table where he'd been sitting, inputting code into his tablet computer.

'All right, Fly-boy,' Brooke whispered to *Punk* as she fitted the top half of his spherical body in place, 'this might tickle!' Using an electric screwdriver, she moved smoothly around the metal sphere, securing the robot's two segments together with a noise that reminded Jackson of the pit crew in a Formula One paddock.

'Clear!' she shouted, dramatically throwing both arms in the air.

'*Tug* ready?' asked Jackson.

'Yessir!' said Brooke, tapping her fist on the chisel-shaped robot's reinforced tungsten-carbide nose.

Jackson began to root around the untidy lab, tipping out boxes of small electric engines, tools and various plastic containers on to the workbench and scrutinizing each object.

'If you're looking to trash the joint, I'm down with that,' Brooke commented wryly. 'But I'm told a TV through a hotel-room window is a lot more therapeutic.'

'I'm looking for an object that they can track.' Jackson continued to talk while he searched. 'We know they can see and use autopilot to follow a route. What I want to know is whether the all-new *thinking Punk* and *Tug* can find and follow their own target, without any help from us.'

Jackson suddenly bent down and pulled a tube of tennis balls from a sports bag under Goulman's desk. 'Perfect!' he said, popping the top off the tube and rolling a bright yellow tennis ball into his hand. 'It's really easy to see. It contrasts with just about everything in the room. And, if I use it with one of these . . .' he slid a tennis racket from Goulman's leather holdall, 'it's really fast!'

*

It was surprising how loud the robots were with their electric-ducted fan thrusters and rotor blades spooled up in the enclosed space of the lab.

'Ready?' Jackson shouted from across the opposite side of the laboratory.

'Let's do it!' called Brooke, her words almost lost in the whirr of the engines.

Jackson opened the terminal window on his tablet screen and entered a final command line – then he touched the ENTER graphic and threw the yellow tennis ball over his shoulder.

Tug's engines screeched as his new programming selected full throttle. Jackson barely had time to dive for cover as the robot made straight for him, ploughing through two 26-inch flatscreens on a workbench and leaving a metal desk lamp snapped clean in half.

Jackson was dusting himself down when he remembered that, as he'd thrown himself out of the way, he'd sent his tablet computer skipping across the concrete floor. He checked in the direction he had thrown the ball and, to his horror, realized that it had disappeared somewhere under a line of metal benches on which sat several expensive-looking pieces of lab equipment. If *Tug* caught sight of the ball, the equipment would be history.

Meanwhile, *Punk* was cautiously zigzagging around benches and chairs, just a few centimetres from the laboratory floor and so Jackson decided, as the errant *Tug* ripped past just millimetres from his head again, that he knew which robot to focus his attention on.

'Now would be a good time to press *Tug*'s stop button!' shouted Brooke, from inside a metal cupboard where she'd taken cover.

Jackson frantically crawled on all fours towards where his tablet computer had landed. At least twice *Tug* made passes low enough to take his head off, and when Jackson eventually saw his computer, he understood why. The hapless tablet was wedged under a line of three metal work-benches – right next to the bright yellow ball's resting place.

Tug was like a dog with a scent, darting erratically across the laboratory, looking for any sign of the brightly coloured object he had been ordered to fetch. *Punk*, on the other hand, was now harmlessly hovering overhead, methodically examining and recording the details of the scene below on his multiple cameras.

Jackson knew that the robot's battery was good for several hours and that the only thing that would stop *Tug* was a line of code from his computer, the very computer that was now within kissing distance of the robot's target. Jackson was only a few metres from his tablet PC when suddenly *Tug*'s engine began to howl. He'd never heard it up close before, but Jackson knew he was listening to *Tug*'s shunt function, sucking up energy in readiness for a strike.

The force with which *Tug* hit the line of metal benches that sheltered the ball and slimline tablet was terrifying.

The middle bench buckled to the point of being virtually folded in half, sending an electron microscope and a particle-size analyser crashing to the ground. As *Tug* wrenched himself free from the wreckage, he left a gouge in the painted concrete floor that exposed the steel mesh and power cables built into the Fire Proof building's concrete structure.

Tug circled overhead and, as the robot took a brief second to decide its next move, Jackson made his. He scrambled under the remaining two benches and reached out for the computer. As he fumbled to grab it, he could hear *Tug* spooling up for another run. This sound he knew. It was the high-pitched whine of one of the 'upgrades' Brooke had given *Tug* since Jackson had moved to Cambridge – an electric turbo that increased *Tug*'s shunting power by three hundred per cent. His next dive for the ball would carry three times the force of the last one!

Jackson didn't even think about it. He grabbed the ball next to his computer and chucked it across the laboratory.

The sound of a thunderous crash filled the room.

The line of four metal cupboards on the other side of the laboratory fell like dominoes. Jackson wasn't sure which one housed Brooke – he just hoped it wasn't one of the two now wrapped round a retreating *Tug*. To make matters worse, the ball's new resting place – by the lockers – hadn't gone unnoticed by *Punk*. He had obviously caught sight of the ball's last known position, in the vicinity of Brooke. Jackson knew he would be using all the technology at his disposal to find or predict his target's location and then would feed that information wirelessly to *Tug*, just as Jackson had programmed him to do.

Jackson recovered his tablet computer and clumsily poked its screen as quickly as he could. If the cumbersome nature of his test control interface hadn't bothered him before, it did now. It was as if every command he entered was accompanied by a bang and a crash from the other side of the room, as *Tug*, aided by *Punk*'s object-tracking predictions, smashed through the remaining lockers in search of his tennis-ball target.

With only one cupboard left standing – the one that Jackson was sure contained Brooke – *Tug*'s engines spooled up for a final strike. It took two lines of the most speedily typed words and numbers that Jackson had ever entered into a computer and, with a microsecond to spare, the noise of the racing electric engines subsided and both robots shut down. *Tug* dropped to the ground and *Punk* performed a perfectly executed hover to land on Brooke's workbench.

Jackson clambered over broken furniture and equipment as he made his way to the mangled cupboards.

'Brooke! Are you OK?' he shouted, overturning desktops and opening the metal doors of the only cupboard still standing.

'That's the last time I play catch with *Tug*!' said Brooke. She was climbing out from underneath the iron stairwell that ran up to ground level from the lab. 'He's a sore loser!'

It took several hours to get the laboratory back into a state that resembled normality. One electron microscope, two desktop computers, four LCD monitors, Goulman's tennis racket, three metal cupboards and one of the workbenches were beyond salvaging. But, with a little welding and the generous use of a hammer, Brooke was able to save most of the furniture.

The experiment had worked; the robots were now clearly capable of thinking for themselves – but if the bedlam of their first test run was to be avoided, a quick and easy way of communicating with them was required. And a means of talking to the machines might just be the thing that could win Singer's AI competition. In Jackson's opinion, Brooke's phones were perfect for controlling *Punk* and *Tug* manually, but for the kind of AI-driven tasks they could now attempt autonomously a means of quickly relaying complex instructions was needed – a language.

Jackson released the socket bolts around *Punk*'s middle and lifted one half of his shell away. He looked like a bowl of noodles, with his power supply unit and flash drive floating in a soup of colourful cables. He unclipped a single block of *Punk*'s flash memory and held it in his hand. It was incredible to think that everything crucial to the robot's functioning – his basic rule set and now the algorithms dedicated to solving every problem his machine brain encountered, which collectively ranged over thousands of lines of code – was contained within a handful of tiny objects the size of Jackson's fingernail.

'Do you think voice recognition might work, Brooke?'

Brooke was picking up papers from the floor with one hand, while texting on her phone with the other. 'Beats me,' she replied wearily.

That's it! thought Jackson. *A quick and easy way of communicating – TEXT messaging!*

Jackson searched the Web for a list of text- and messenger-friendly words and emoticons. He then painstakingly went through each word and assigned it a numerical value from 0 to 9 for factors such as the word's emotional weight and its importance in a mission situation.

		Emotion	MissionValue	Danger
IDK	(I don't know)	3	9	7
fO_o	(Scratch head)	3	8	6
?_?	(Confused)	8	9	8
(o_#)	(Bruised)	7	8	8
(#_#)	(Beaten)	9	9	9
X-(	(Brain-dead)	8	8	6
OIC	(Oh, I see)	7	7	8

(>_~)	(Suspicious)	7	9	9
XLNT	(Excellent)	8	1	0
ROFL	(Roll on floor laughing)	9	0	0
LOL	(Laugh out loud)	7	0	0
°-°	(Shocked)	8	7	3
(ò.ó)	(Angry)	8	8	8
TY	(Thank you)	8	5	0
NP	(No problem)	2	3	0
UR	(your/you're)	2	7	1
PLS	(Please)	5	7	3
CYA	(See you)	6	0	0
SRY	(sorry)9	7	5	
TBC	(to be continued)	6	7	2
NM	(Nothing much)	3	3	3
NVM	(Never mind)	6	3	0
W/E	(Whatever)	8	5	2
Q(-_-)P	(Thumbs-down)	8	5	3
B(~_^)D	(Thumbs-up)	8	5	3
GR8	(Great)9	5	0	
FYI	(For your info)	4	9	7
FTW	(For the win)	4	9	8
RUOK	(Are you OK?)	8	9	6
SUP	(What's up?)	6	8	6
D/Q	(Disconnected)	1	8	8
@_'-'	(Snail slow)	6	5	1
:-&	(Tongue-tied)	5	3	3

Then Jackson started to add all the phrases he could think of that might help with *Punk* and *Tug*'s specific operational requirements, converting them into text-speak as he went; so phrases like HOVER and TOP SPEED became 'HVR' and 'TP SPD'. After some time, Jackson had created a sizeable language database with each phrase allotted a series of values, which would enable *Punk* and *Tug* to both understand and speak in text-message shorthand.

He considered 'IDK', the shorthand response for the phrase 'I don't know', to be of medium emotional significance, but of great mission importance, based on the idea that if a robot had no clue how to respond to a problem or a lack of awareness about the severity of a situation, it could quickly lead to trouble. For example, if Jackson asked *Tug* if the light on an explosive device was on and he replied 'IDK', it was reasonable to assume that the device might go off.

Jackson also mixed emoticons into the list, to give *Tug* and *Punk* as wide a range of expression as possible. So 'fO_o', which looked like someone scratching their head, meant roughly the same as 'IDK', but was considered less mission critical because it suggested that, with a little more thinking time, the robots might come up with an answer.

By 9 p.m. the list was complete. Jackson reassembled *Punk* and installed the list, along with several hundred lines of operating code, into both robots.

Punk sat on the desk, the spikes on his underside at

half extension forming a triangle of stunted prongs on which he rested. His blue lights glowed behind the thin window of bulletproof transparent polycarbonate plastic on the front of his metal body. *Well, he's awake*, Jackson thought. *Let's see if he can speak.*

Brooke wandered over to see what was happening as Jackson typed a message into his phone's messaging application: 'SYSTM CHCK PLS'.

Almost immediately, the temperature of Jackson's phone peaked as *Punk*'s reply appeared on its surface: 'Y SUP (>_~)'.

Brooke burst out laughing. 'Well, I'll be darned. All those hours of programming and we got ourselves a robot with attitude.'

She grabbed the handset from Jackson and speedily punched in a message: 'NTHNG UP. SYSTM CHCK PLS!'

'NP,' replied *Punk*, followed by a list of system information that crowded the surface of the smartphone:

```
MACHINE ID: PNK
SYSTM VERSN: LNX 17.5.4
925Z883508FOP2 OK
TXT-SPEAK ENGN: V1.0 OK
NTWRKNG: AUTO OK
FRWLL: OK
NMBR OF PRCSSRS: 16 OK
NMBR OF CRS: 128 OK
```

```
COOLNG: OK
MMRY: 2 TB
PRMRY BTTRY: 80%
RSRV BTTRY: 100%
MAIN DRV SRV: OK
SCNDRY DRV: OK
DFNC FRMWRK: PRMD
COL SNSR: OFF
```

Jackson mentally translated the information showing on his phone:

Machine ID: PUNK
System Version: Linux 17.5.4 (925)Z883508F0P2 OK
Text-Speak Engine: V1.0 OK
Networking: Automatic OK
Firewall: OK
Number of Processors: 16 OK
Number of Cores: 128 OK
Cooling: OK
Memory: 2 TB
Primary Battery: 80%
Reserve Battery: 100%
Main Drive Servo: OK
Secondary Drive: OK
Defence Framework: Primed
Collision Sensor: Off

'Wow!' Jackson snorted. 'He's talking my language!'

'Now let's do something a little more adventurous with him,' said Brooke.

She typed 'HVR' and sent it.

There was a barely perceivable pulse from behind *Punk*'s screen, followed by the noise of the ducted fans around the spherical robot's shell spooling up. Suddenly a spike shot upwards from the top of *Punk* and three rotor blades flicked out and snapped into place while simultaneously beginning to turn.

Punk began to rise slowly into the air, short blasts from the fan vents helping to stabilize him in a firm hover.

'Well, Master Chief! You've done excelled yourself,' said Brooke, slapping Jackson heartily on the shoulder. 'Now I suggest you go get some shut-eye. Dad is testing *Verne* in waters off Martha's Vineyard tomorrow and he wants you there!'

The streets of Cambridge, Massachusetts, were friendly. Jackson had thought that when he'd just arrived and taken his first walk in America. They seemed especially amiable this evening, softened in the warm glow of the streetlamps, alive with smiley-faced students who congregated outside coffee shops and restaurants and thrift stores open late.

A gang of fire-fighters were polishing a gleaming red-and-chrome fire truck they'd parked across the pavement outside their station, while over the road in a small triangular piazza, a young man with a really large afro haircut was plucking a guitar in front of a couple of pretty girls who were giving him the eye from behind thick textbooks.

This warm, tranquil evening had lulled Jackson into pushing his bike home so that he could enjoy the last moments of summer. And it had also allowed him to spot the blacked-out van. Jackson stopped and stared at it from across the street. It had shaded windows and a sliding door on the side, and he could just make out two figures through the front windscreen.

Jackson memorized the number plate – it was easy because it contained 204, which he knew was a pyramidal number and the number of different squares on a chessboard. Then he stopped himself. What was he doing? This was the kind of paranoia he'd got used to when he thought Lear's men might come for him – but that was over a year ago. Still, Jackson knew that once you'd made the decision to get involved with a secret organization like MeX, you didn't get to choose when to feel ordinary again. Even when that organization was a year since dead, you had to settle for sleepless nights and paranoia.

Jackson climbed on to his bike and started to pedal. He tried to think what to do. *If I see the van again, then I'll . . . do what exactly?* Last time he'd felt like this, when he thought men in a black Range Rover were stalking him around the streets of Peckham, Brooke had actually been kidnapped. But he had nothing to fear now – Lear was dead. He put it down to a glitch in the code that ran his head – the result of too long spent talking to robots.

The elevator in his dorm building was broken again. He had started up the stairs, carrying his bike, when the porter called out: 'You'll be wanting this, Mr Farley!' It was the first time the old man had spoken to him. He shuffled slowly up to Jackson, wearing the full doorman's regalia of long green trench coat with gold buttons and braid, white hat and gloves, and handed him a FedEx box.

Jackson struggled up the stairs with the bike and box, before falling clumsily into his room. He dived straight over his bike and on to his bed to rip the parcel open.

He tipped the parcel upside down and let its contents fall on to his duvet. There was a stack of photographs held together by a rubber band, a copy of the *Peckham News* folded at the obituaries page, several coloured-pencil drawings of cars and aircraft, which Jackson remembered doing when he was younger, a folded paper menu for a restaurant called the Shanghai Star, a flowery invitation to a christening, which on closer inspection Jackson saw was his own, and three red linen-covered diaries, each with the year embossed in gold. Finally, he also spotted an envelope with 'Jackson' written on it in a scrawl, which he recognized as his dad's.

Jackson opened the envelope first and pulled out a letter.

Dear Jackson,

It was great to receive your email, son. Hope you don't mind my old-fashioned snail mail! You are right, I was feeling really down. Mrs Delee from flat 27 said she thought I was right off colour. She's been leaving me meals, and yesterday she posted a pamphlet through my door about swine flu!

As soon as I arrived at Heathrow, I wanted to get straight back on a plane and come back to Boston. I guess the thought that you might beat me up kept me in England. That, and the fact that you have such good people around you.

Anyway, I'm not very good at this letter-writing stuff so I'll get to the point. I am truly sorry for handling things the way I did. Your mother would have killed me. I'm bad at the emotional things and I kept putting it off and putting it off. Anyway, now you know. But you should also know that I love you and it changes nothing between you and me.

By the way, I know why you want your mum's stuff. You want to try and find out who your biological father is. It's OK, son, I understand. I've put her things in this parcel. I've never been able to bring myself to read her diaries but if you think it'll help you through this, it's fine with me – I know you'll look after them. But also look after yourself. I've asked Professor English to keep an eye on you. Don't go ringing any strangers up and asking them if they're missing a son! If you need any help just email me, or ring from the phone in the prof's office.

I miss you loads.

Love, <u>DAD</u>

PS I hope you've been enjoying using your watch!

Jackson smiled to himself – it was a relief to be back on good terms with his dad. He jumped off the bed and picked up his binary watch from his desk. He placed it on his wrist – for the first time. He had been so angry with his dad that he hadn't worn it. But that had faded now. Jackson looked at the watch. A watch that requires binary addition in order to reveal the time – *genius!*

Jackson got himself a bowl of cereal and sat on the bed to look at the menu next. The Shanghai Star was the restaurant his mum loved most in the world. As he opened it, he noticed that three dishes were circled in pencil. He didn't need to read the menu to know they were her favourites, highlighted so his dad could get the takeaway order right: Crispy Sesame Shrimp, Broccoli in Garlic Sauce and Green Tea Ice Cream. Jackson still knew the order by heart. When it had been his turn to phone up, he would conjure up the numbers down the side of the menu: *'A 276, a 380 and two scoops of 703, please.'*

Next he picked up the first of the red diaries. He remembered seeing his mother writing in one of them and recognized the black elastic-material strap she would snap over it when she'd finished. Each page represented one day and was sub-divided into time slots from 7 a.m. to 7 p.m. Jackson found the first entry on the page for 7 January. His mother had all but ignored the lines on the page and the time slots, and had just written in big red letters in the middle of the page:

Thursday 7 January

I'M WRITING A DIARY! HURRAH!

Never thought I was the diary-keeping kind. Guess I'm about to find out. I was given this diary by Moe, so it would be rude not to try and write something down.

Below the entry, which was circled by red stars, was a detailed drawing of a Japanese girl. The drawing, which showed a girl with delicate doll-like features and long hair held in a bunch by two sticks, was labelled 'Moe x'.

Jackson leafed through the pages of his mum's Oxford life, ignoring entries about netball practice, arguments with her roommate, who he quickly worked out was this Moe, shopping lists and dates when maths assignments were due in. He took an interest when she mentioned her course topics, quickly checked her workings when he came across them and laughed out loud at a cartoon she had sketched suggesting that quantum theory might be to blame for her always having odd socks. And Jackson noted the mention of her beginning a third year of Japanese-language night class with a Professor Kinjo – he remembered that speaking Japanese had always been one of his mum's party tricks.

He also read the rough bits of poems she intended to write up at some later date. These fascinated Jackson because he had a notepad filled with his mother's poetry, which his father had given him after her death.

The first page that really caught his attention had two words circled at the bottom.

Friday 2 April

Remind Moe it's her turn to do the laundry! (She always forgets!!!!)

7 p.m. Christ Church – Spectral Theory of Random Matrices lecture (Tell me I'm not dedicated!)

*Phone Pope

For a moment Jackson couldn't quite place the name, Pope, knowing that he'd heard it before, but then he remembered seeing the picture from the university website – Lumpy, D. Alexander and Mr Pope, the names of the three people who, along with his mother, made up the Oxford University maths team.

He continued to skim through the diary, paying less heed to entries about day-to-day stuff, but taking in all the references to Mr Pope, which seemed to increase in frequency.

Tuesday 8 June

I'M SO ANGRY!

Popey got mad at me today! Although I did lose it for us against the Cambridge team. What is it about diophantine equations that turns me into such a doofus?! Still, he didn't need to be soooo rude! Am I a good judge of character?

Wednesday 9 June

Revision really sucks!

Differentional Geometry and Einstein Spaces. Grrrr!

$E = mc^2$

$D = sr^2$

Depression $= (summer \times revision)^2$

Flowers. Lots of Flowers, from the Pope. I think I'll forgive him (but I'll let him sweat it out a little first!)

Monday 14 June

Shifting beams throw my rose window
Thaw the cells off every sinew
But I'm stone chilled and racked with fear
AS THE DREADED EXAMS ARE FINALLY HERE!

Mr Pope has had an offer from a big London city firm.

To Do List:

- *Pass exams with flying colours!*
- *Find a job!!!!*
- *Have a great life*

Wednesday 16 June

☹

4 p.m. Drinks with Prof. Kinjo. I'll really miss Japanese class :-(
Shikatanai (That's life!)
6 till early hours – Yet More Revision!!!

Thursday 17 June

Revised with Popey tonight. Can't believe he's off to start his job next week. We were both a bit sad. Friends forever xxx

Did I mention I was revising?!!?

Friday 18 June
EXAMS

Thursday 24 June
EXAMS

Friday 25 June
EXAMS

Saturday 26 June
☺

FREEDOM :-)

This is what freedom looks like:

11 a.m. – Hair appointment (I know, get me!)

12 p.m. – Me and Moe sunbathe.

4 p.m. – Tea with maths fellows of Jesus.

5 p.m. – Mysterious meeting with Prof. Kinjo! Not really – think he just wants to say bye – me being <u>star Japanese student!</u> :-)

7 p.m. – Meet gang – Lumpy, Alexander, Moe's lot. No Popey, though – as he's already started his job!

10 p.m. – Fireworks at Christ Church.

Jackson was about to fire up his tablet and look again at the maths team photo. He was particularly keen to look at Popey again as she'd seemed quite keen on him. Then he spotted the pack of photos that had come in his dad's package and started to shuffle through those instead.

He flicked through a procession of school photos of himself in uniform and shamefully noted that his haircut had hardly changed in five years of school photographs. There was a Polaroid of him, his mum and his dad at home, and snaps of his parents cuddling on the sofa. Then he came across several older photographs that Jackson suspected were taken in Oxford. There were two of his mum dancing around in a kitchen with a Japanese girl he recognized as Moe, from the drawing in his mum's diary, and there were several more of the two girls together, one of which showed them having a picnic with the members of the maths team. The picture wasn't very clear, but Mr Pope's distinctive baseball cap and shades were unmistakable. And, unless Jackson was imagining things, he and his mum were pressed up against each other for the photo and laughing.

Jackson wasn't sure how he felt about the picture, with his mother cuddling up to someone who wasn't his dad. Jackson decided it was best just to press on.

He opened the next diary. It was three years after the previous one and covered two years. He found little

of interest in the first few months beyond appoint-
ments with names he didn't recognize, and a few
comments that suggested she was working in an office.
Then he came to an entry in April.

Thursday 11 April

*5 p.m. – Interviewing for a position in another department.
Should be able to use my Japanese translation skills.*

Can't believe I've been at The Jam for six months ...

The Jam Company! As a kid, Jackson had imagined the
place his mother worked as a kind of Charlie Wonka's
Chocolate Factory – but with jam. He'd never thought
that her job there – in the accounts department – required
her to speak Japanese.

He continued to look through the diary. To begin with
the entries were a lot sparser than in the previous diary.
There were one or two brief entries a month – meeting
times at The Jam, notes for a complaint about the state
of the bus station at Cheltenham where Jackson remembered she used to commute to daily for her job. One entry
made Jackson stop and re-read it a few times.

Friday 23 August

Sometimes I wonder whose side we're on!

Inside the page was a return bus ticket to Cheltenham. It was a strange entry, Jackson thought, because he couldn't imagine what she meant by it.

The bus ticket gave him an idea and he started up the browser on his tablet computer and did a search for The Jam Company in Cheltenham. Nothing caught his attention. Now he came to think of it, he didn't remember any details about the place other than its name and that she travelled to Cheltenham and back to work there. So why wasn't it coming up in the search?

To Jackson and his dad she'd always referred to it as The Jam Company. But once or twice in the pages of her diary, she'd used a nickname – The Jam.

Jackson entered 'The Jam +Cheltenham'. A reference to Chilli Jam came up first, followed by some music venues. He waded through several pages of links that inspired nothing but frustration, then, from nowhere, a reference that mentioned GCHQ. Jackson knew straightaway what GCHQ was. It featured heavily in one of his favourite books – *The Bletchley Bomb*. The book, which had belonged to his grandfather, told the story of codebreaking in the Second World War. GCHQ was the name of the British government's code-cracking headquarters.

Jackson clicked on the link. It led to a page filled with information about what it called the government's centre for communications. Jackson's eye was drawn to one particular sentence:

> Among insiders, the 'company' has gained the nickname 'The Jam' because the new GCHQ building is shaped like a doughnut and what goes on inside it is the jam in the doughnut.

One part of Jackson was astonished. If he understood things correctly, his mother had worked for the British government's code-cracking department in Cheltenham and not a factory making preserves. But another part of him found it made perfect sense – she had been a brilliant mathematician and had even written in code the Pi poem that she'd given to Jackson on his seventh birthday. It was a code that he'd had to break in order to receive his present.

He read on and slowly the picture of his mother's job as a code-breaker began to form. She translated phone calls between Japan and Britain and, although Jackson wasn't sure who the phone calls were between or why she had to translate them, it was clear that she was passing on her findings up the line at GCHQ. But if that wasn't enough of a shock for Jackson, then the following entries definitely were.

Thursday 24 October

Mr Yakimoto coming to London. And I discovered it. ME!

Friday 25 October

*Popey works for us! I can't believe it. The boss just introduced
him into one of our meetings.*

Thursday 7 November

*Been working with Mr Pope all week. He's been working for
us in our 'London Office' since he left Oxford.
Oh, and he invited me to dinner!*

Wednesday 13 November

Everything lovely with Popey.

Tuesday 19 November

*I'm very worried!
They've assigned Popey to the Yakimoto job.*

Monday 25 November

*My Mr Pope meets Yakimoto in ten weeks.
I have to listen in and tell the boss when to move in.*

Jackson noticed a distinct lack of anything written in the diary
for several weeks.

Monday 10 February

*Too upset to have written in my diary until now.
They've taken Popey.
I can hardly write his name without crying.*

Thursday 10 February

News from Japan not good. Had confirmation that Popey was taken there.

I blame myself – I can't help it.

I will always treasure the night we spent together before he met that man.

Thursday 6 March

Still no news from Japan company contact.

Tuesday 18 March

12 p.m., St Stephens – Memorial Service for Popey.

Thursday 27 March

I'm PREGNANT.

Hard to get my head around.

I can't believe Popey will never meet his child.

Jackson felt numb. His mother's discovery of her pregnancy – 27 March – was seven months before Jackson was born. She was pregnant, with him! It followed that there in the pages of his mother's diary was the identity of his real father – Mr Pope, Popey from her university days. But while it was the one piece of knowledge he thought he wanted to know more than anything else, any relief it might have given him had been crushed by the revelation that followed – his real father was dead. The cryptic understatement of his mother's diary entries made the precise chain of events difficult to decipher, but, as Jackson understood it, his mum and Mr Pope were involved in some kind of sting operation involving a Japanese man called Mr Yakimoto – an operation that had ended with the abduction and death of Mr Pope in Japan.

Jackson grasped the third and final diary in his hands. He'd see what the Web would throw up about Yakimoto later, but right now he was desperate to read on.

He looked at the year stamped in gold on the front cover. It was a full ten years on from the end of the previous diary. It was the year his mother died.

Jackson flicked slowly through the entries, not wanting to reach the end of this final diary, knowing what it would bring. The first few months were ordinary: a few notes about meetings at The Jam to pay bills, a nice sketch of Jackson's dad, who Jackson was somehow relieved to read was now part of their lives, watching TV. About halfway through his mother's routine scribbles took a disturbing turn.

Friday 27 April
Yakimoto is coming back!

Friday 11 May
I've been asked to consult on the Yakimoto meet.
I don't know if I can bring myself to take part …

Monday 21 May

I'm in! I'm doing it. And this time we'll get him!

Thursday 24 May

Feeling guilty. I've been working silly hours.
Jackson is very sweet about it, but I know he hates me coming in so late.

Tuesday 12 June

Three days to go.
I've listened to as much phone traffic as I can. It's out of my hands now.
This one's for you, Popey.

Friday 15 June

Tried to sleep but couldn't . . .
Think I was followed home. I'll tell my department head tomorrow.

This entry was accompanied by a doodle of a Japanese man. Jackson's mother had used up lots of ink from her biro on his long flowing black hair. His round spectacles had been inked in so they looked shaded in blue, and his angular face gave him a harsh appearance. Jackson was in no doubt it was Yakimoto.

Jackson turned over the page, but he knew he would find nothing. Saturday 16 June. The date was seared into his memory. It was the date of his mother's death.

Up until this moment, Jackson had believed his mother had been killed in a hit and run. Now he was facing a new and even more hideous truth – that she had been murdered by the same man who had killed his real father.

CHAPTER 12

Jackson had a few more minutes to ponder over the wording of the email.

Brooke was meant to have collected him from outside Simmons Hall at 8 a.m. for their trip to the island of Martha's Vineyard. Jackson was waiting outside when she called at 8.15 to say she was still packing gear with her father and would be an hour late. Jackson had offered to help out, but she'd told him J.P. was in one of his moods and while she could not escape it he could.

Jackson sat on the pavement outside the dorm building, happy to have a spare hour to continue his research into Yakimoto. It felt like he'd read everything there was to know about every Mr Yakimoto in Japan last night. He'd narrowed his search down to one man who fitted the bill – a businessman who had been investigated many times for alleged links to the Yakuza, apparently Japan's most famous criminal organization. But by the time Jackson had finally put his head down, at around 5 a.m., the information he'd managed to find on his parents' mysterious killer was, at best, sketchy.

In spite of the little amount of sleep he'd managed to get, he had woken up with a plan. His search for the Japanese gangster might be proving difficult – but he knew someone who might have more luck.

He finished his email to the Kojima twins and touched SEND.

What most impressed Jackson about the Englishs' fifteen-bedroom beachside house on the island of Martha's Vineyard was Brooke's tepee.

The tall conical structure sat at the end of a long lawn, just a few metres from a small private beach. It was covered with sections of grass matting and animal pelts that spiralled down from a twig crown, giving it the appearance of a helter-skelter.

'It's an exact replica of the tepees used by the Wampanoag Indians, the original inhabitants of this island. My friend John is a direct descendant of one of the tribes. He helped me build it.'

The island was little more than an hour from Boston by boat and yet, looking out from the sand towards the flat expanse of sunset-orange ocean, Jackson imagined he could have been a castaway on a desert island.

'I never really thought about Indians living on islands,' said Jackson.

Brooke smiled. 'They still live here! John and his family

live on a reservation up on the peninsula. Many people believe the Wampanoag are the heart of the island. When the early settlers chased many of them off Martha's Vineyard, strange things started to happen like floods and violent storms. They've been welcome here ever since.'

It was *so* Brooke, thought Jackson, to have the run of a beautiful house but choose to sleep in a tepee.

It wasn't hard to see why. It was very peaceful here, even the waves were whisper quiet, lapping on to the beach almost apologetically, a few metres from where the two of them sat. Jackson dug his toes into the sand. It was only warm on the surface, cold underneath. A bit like how he felt right now, to tell the truth. The AI project had eventually turned out well and he was glad to be here on the island to help Brooke and J.P., but underneath all he could think about was what had happened to his mother. He felt numb.

It must have showed on his face.

'Whatever is going on between you and your dad,' Brooke remarked softly, 'you know you can always talk about it to me if you need to.'

'He's not my real dad,' said Jackson firmly. 'That's what he had to tell me.'

At first, Brooke said nothing, but Jackson could see the surprise in her eyes.

'Do you know who is?' asked Brooke, eventually breaking the silence.

Brooke was his best friend, and part of Jackson desperately wanted to tell her – to let out all the shocking things he'd found out in the last couple of days. But there was so much he didn't know himself. Who had Mr Pope been anyway, when he was alive? He'd done a search on his name last night and found nothing. And then there was Mr Yakimoto – even thinking of his name made Jackson feel sick to the pit of his stomach. No, he couldn't tell Brooke anything just yet. Not until he knew more himself – it was easier that way.

'I'm not entirely sure who he is, Brooke – but I'm working on it.'

'OK. But if there's anything I can do to help –'

'Like I said,' responded Jackson, cutting Brooke off, 'I'm working on it.'

The sea was glassy smooth. If it wasn't for the keel of J.P.'s ship, *The Oceanaut*, slicing through it at an impressive rate of knots, Jackson believed its surface would be undisturbed until it touched Europe.

Things aboard the boat were busy, though. Goulman had called in sick yesterday, much to J.P.'s annoyance, and the professor had drafted in the son of a friend who introduced himself as Matty. J.P., Jackson and the new guy were busy readying *Verne*. They hoisted the spherical white robot on to the end of a small crane which swung out over the stern of the boat, and began running final tests via an indestructible-looking rubberized tablet PC which was plugged into *Verne*'s belly by a thick red cable.

Getting *Verne* to the crane had been a challenge – *Verne* was a lot heavier than Jackson had expected. J.P. had explained that, in order to keep the remote underwater machine balanced when under the sea, *Verne* needed to carry a lot of weight. Matty had complained that he was suffering from a dodgy back and J.P. was too intent on directing manoeuvres to be of any real help, so Jackson had spent most of the half-hour journey from Edgartown inching the 130-kilogram machine across the deck. If Salty, the boat's captain, and quite possibly the strongest old-age pensioner Jackson had ever seen, hadn't come to his aid, J.P.'s experimental aquatic robot might well still be sitting in his crate.

Salty had later invited Jackson to join him on the 'flying bridge'.

'I'm sorry, but I don't know much about boating,' said Jackson. 'What's a flying bridge when it's at home?'

'You know what a crow's-nest is?' said the old man, through all of three teeth and a white beard that clung to his face and neck like a barnacle.

'I do! It's the bit at the top of a ship's mast that you stand in and shout when you see the pirates coming!'

Salty burst out laughing and then proceeded to cough and splutter before forming a mouthful of something foul, which he promptly spat over the side of the open platform.

'Brooke said you were funny, lad!'

'Oh, did she? What did she say?'

'That you have the smarts to match any of the Doc's hangers-on, but an accent that makes you sound as dumb as a crayfish.'

'Are crayfish dumb?'

'God-awful stupid! They'll eat the hook off your line.'

'Is there such a thing as a clever fish?'

Salty swivelled round in his fighting chair, keeping one hand on the ship's chrome wheel. 'Don't go thinking we're anything more than guests out here, boy. There's a million creatures below us right now who is wily enough to drag us down there to join 'em, if they ever feel the need.'

It was an old sea dog talking and Jackson felt a shiver down his back.

Brooke's voice brought him right back to reality. 'Don't tell me, you've found someone gullible enough to listen to your rubbish!'

Jackson looked down on to the deck below and saw Brooke standing there, the front of her head covered by a pair of very large goggles. They were part of a virtual reality headset.

'You like my new shades?' said Brooke.

'I've heard that *big* is in, so you'll be OK with those,' replied Jackson.

'They come with a matching glove,' said Brooke, holding up what looked like the glove from a wetsuit. It was attached to the headset via a bright yellow hose. 'It's completely waterproof. The idea is that whoever is driving *Verne* has the choice of doing it from the deck of the boat, or jumping into the water to join him. Wanna try it on?'

Brooke slipped the goggles over Jackson's head. Instantly he could see a great expanse of ocean and white frothy wash, which he guessed was *Verne*'s current view over the back of the vessel.

'The display can work as a simple video camera,' Brooke continued. 'Or with acoustic imaging in zero-visibility conditions.'

'Jeepers, girl! Would you stop talking like a computer,' Salty scolded from up on the bridge.

'It means you can drive *Verne* in pitch black, Salty. A bit like you do, when you fall asleep at the helm.'

There was a splutter of laughter from J.P.'s direction.

'Now you wouldn't be gettin' into a quarrel with an old man who knows enough about you to turn that pretty little face of yours as red as the hair on your head?'

'This could be interesting,' said Jackson.

'You keep quiet, old man, or I'll refuse to fix the engine in this junk bucket next time she's had enough of you!'

Salty leaned over the edge of the bridge and whispered down to Brooke and Jackson. 'And then I might have to tell of the time you forgot to collect your pappy's car from off the beach. I wonder how he'd take the news that his precious sports car wasn't thieved, but was swallowed up by the ocean?'

'How did you know that?' hissed an amazed Brooke, looking carefully behind to make sure her father wasn't in earshot.

'Old Salty knows a lot of things,' winked the old fisherman. And Jackson believed him.

Half an hour later *The Oceanaut* had shut down her engines and was drifting gently in the calm sea. J.P. checked the vessel's location on the GPS readout on his tablet computer. 'This is it,' said the professor. 'OK, Matty, prep her for a dive.'

Jackson scanned the horizon in all directions. They were so far out now that neither the coast nor the boats that hung around the entrance to Edgartown were visible. All that broke up the shimmering expanse of blue were the ripples created by the odd tern that dived for food, and the distant outline of a yacht.

'This is my dad's preferred testing spot,' said Brooke. 'There's a series of large rocks and trenches on the seabed here which are perfect for doing manoeuvrability and depth tests. Salty has brought us here a hundred times. He swears he navigates by nothing more than smell.'

'*Verne* is checked and ready,' said J.P. 'How about you, Brooke?'

J.P. stood in the cabin at the centre of the boat. The rest of the group had assembled by the cabin's doorway to listen to his briefing. Jackson thought Brooke looked hilarious, leaning against the boat's railings in flip-flops, flowery Bermuda shorts and a large high-tech VR helmet on her head. 'All systems are go, Boss,' was her muffled reply.

'*Verne* will be operating here on the seabed at a depth of around one hundred metres,' J.P. said as he commenced his briefing. 'Our primary task is to test his new augmented display and make sure he responds properly to all of Brooke's inputs. Last time we were here we mapped the position of a few objects of interest.'

'Buried treasure,' Brooke whispered to Jackson, with an air of mystery.

'Discarded scuba dive tanks to be precise,' continued the professor. 'The important thing is that we know their precise location on the ocean floor so we can use them as markers for *Verne*'s augmented display. In order to do that, once we reach the ocean floor, I'll ask Brooke to turn *Verne*'s video cameras off. From that point on, she'll be flying using just this computer-generated scan of the ocean floor.'

J.P. turned one of the large flatscreen monitors in the cabin towards the group. It showed a vivid image of what looked like an aerial view of a mountain range, with bright green peaks and valleys of dark red. In one of the red trenches, Jackson could see a cluster of four wire-framed pill-shaped objects.

'Are those the scuba tanks?' he asked, pointing at the tiny pills on the screen.

'They sure are. If Brooke can guide *Verne* to the bottles and have him pick one of them up, using just this virtual map, then we'll be confident the augmented display can work in total blackout.'

'And what does this colour represent?' said Jackson, referring to a dark reddish-purple area at the top of the screen.

'Swallow Hole,' said Salty, with his eyes wide. 'She'll swallow you up as easy as you can say her name.'

'It's one of several deep-water trenches in this part of the Atlantic Ocean,' said J.P., smiling. 'Salty likes to get lyrical about its reputation for having sucked many sailors and their ships down to their doom. But we won't be going anywhere near it today.'

'Shipwrecks? Cool. Couldn't you use *Verne* to investigate or is it too deep down there?' asked Jackson.

'Nothing's too deep for *Verne*. He's designed to operate in the deep ocean, at depths as low as 10,000 metres,' said J.P.

'The pressure must be incredible down there!' said Jackson.

'Roughly 16,000 pounds per square inch.'

'That's the equivalent of stacking three *Tin Lizzie*s on your little toe,' said Brooke.

'He must be pretty tough then,' murmured Jackson,

glancing over to the white robot sphere swinging gently in its cradle.

'Ceramics on the outside – syntactic foam on the inside,' said Brooke. 'The outer shell is about the only material strong enough to withstand the enormous forces pressing in on *Verne* at those depths. The foam inside is a super-strong mix of metal and polymer filled with hollow particles called micro-balloons. The tiny balloons allow *Verne* to float in the water.'

'OK, guys, science lesson over, we've got work to do,' interrupted J.P. 'Matty, get *Verne* into the water! Salty, I need you to keep *The Oceanaut* steady against the tide.'

'Aye, aye. She'll not move, Doc.'

'Jackson, you're our numbers man.' J.P. handed Jackson his tablet computer. 'There are four diving cylinders down there. I want you to keep an eye on the position we have mapped for them and cross-reference it with Brooke's virtual readout. You can see what Brooke's VR helmet is showing on the tablet screen.'

'Ain't that summat one of yer computer machines could do?' asked Salty.

'Jackson *is* a computer,' said Brooke.

Jackson sized up the device he'd been handed. It was about the size of an A4 pad, with black-and-yellow rubber around its edges. He touched its screen and instantly the 10.4-inch OLED display showed the bright white hull and shiny chrome steps at the back of the boat, before being filled with crystal blue as *Verne* was lowered into the water.

Jackson glanced in Brooke's direction. She was sitting in a deckchair in the middle of the deck, forming abstract shapes with her gloved hand. He could see the changing view from *Verne* on the tablet computer screen as the machine responded to her bizarre sign language and rolled a full circle while descending.

'Less of the freestyle, please, honey. Keep it nice and smooth.' J.P. was inside the cabin watching the feeds from *Verne* on several large flatscreens.

Now the boat was stationary, the cooling breeze from their journey out here had been replaced by waves of heat that bounced up from the sparkling water. But even in the bright September sun, the details on the tablet's touch-screen were very clear. The wide-angle lens from the camera mounted on *Verne*'s nose showed a welcoming bright blue world. Clouds of silver fish flashed in coordinated turns against the sand. Flanking the beltway of seabed were row after row of light-grey rocks, which Jackson thought looked very similar to the scan J.P. had shown them. It was hard to get a sense of scale from the high-definition video feed, but from the height of the tall green weeds that rose from them and billowed in the current, the biggest of the rocks was taller than a house.

It took only a few minutes for Brooke to guide *Verne* to the sea floor, at which point she levelled him out and flew him less than a metre above the sand. The view from the ball-shaped machine reminded Jackson of the robotic missions he and Brooke had flown for MeX. The volcanic gullies and peaks were like miniature versions of the hills and valleys of Ukraine and Moldova they had passed on their way to their final encounter with Lear. It was a ride he'd relived many times in his dreams, sometimes waking in a sweat as ghoulish flying saucers stalked him through the branches of a dark forest, or villagers ran screaming as Jackson lost control of *Tug* and smashed him through row upon row of cottages and farmhouses. This time, however, Jackson wasn't scared. He had rarely seen anything as beautiful as the underwater moonscape through which *Verne* was gliding.

'Numbers, Farley?' called J.P.

Towards the top of his screen, Jackson could see a range of digits which represented *Verne*'s speed, his baro-metric altitude, which was calculated by measuring changes in the pressure of the water around him, the elapsed time since leaving the boat, his rate of climb or descent in metres per second and four sets of descending six-figure numbers which Jackson took to be the distances to the cluster of diver's tanks. 'He's about four hundred metres from the target zone.'

'OK, Brooke, you happy to switch to the virtual view?' J.P. asked.

'But it's so beautiful down there, why would you wanna go spoil it?' replied Brooke.

The view from inside Brooke's helmet instantly snapped from an iridescent blue underwater wonderland to the stark electric greens, yellows and reds of *Verne*'s acoustic seabed scan. 'Which joker just turned the lights out in my aquarium?' she said.

Jackson still had the feed from *Verne*'s cameras, but was able to jump between it and the seabed scan that Brooke was seeing by touching the VIEW tab. And, as he did so, he noticed an instant change in the values at the top of the screen.

To a casual observer, it would have seemed impossible to discern the minute differences in the reams of quickly changing digits that crowned the two views. But in Jackson's finely tuned numerical brain, the figures, which denoted *Verne*'s height, speed and direction, were not consistent. In the way a baseball player sees the curve in the flight of a ball when the rest of us see a straight line, or a composer computes all the possible combinations of notes before selecting the least expected one, Jackson sensed that the real position of *Verne* in the water was roughly 3.5 millimetres north by north-east of the position the virtual display had him in.

'By my reckoning, if Brooke continues in her current direction, *Verne* will be about 1.7 metres wide of the target zone when he reaches it. You need to recalibrate the virtual display,' Jackson called out, pausing to think for moment. 'Add three decimal seconds to the longitude axis and take away two decimal seconds from the latitude axis.'

'I'll be damned! The boy's a talking compass!' Salty shouted from his vantage point on the bridge.

'I told you he was good,' laughed Brooke.

'OK, I've made the corrections. Brooke, you're cleared to retrieve the tanks now. Take it nice and easy. Remember, they're probably still pressurized. We don't want any accidents.'

CHAPTER 13

The view from inside Brooke's headset looked just like a video game. The seabed was represented by an intricate mesh of electric-blue lines that traced the precise contours of the ocean floor, and virtual waves rolled along the top of her display. Glinting in the distance were six bright white pill-shaped objects, graphical renderings of the discarded scuba tanks she was aiming for.

Brooke moved her gloved hand through a series of delicate gestures and *Verne* slowly turned away from the tanks and started to descend. Almost instantaneously J.P.'s voice came over the intercom.

'Do we have a problem, Brooke?'

'No, Dad, I just think that if this is supposed to be a test of *Verne*, that's exactly what we should be doing.'

As she spoke, she twisted her wrist and the robot gracefully descended towards a deep ravine with steep rock sides.

'Brooke, I'd prefer that you made straight for the tanks, please.'

'Dad, we haven't really tested this acoustic display, and a little sightseeing excursion is the perfect way to do it. Just trust me.'

'OK, but I want you over to those scuba tanks in less than a minute,' urged her father.

Jackson watched the screen in his hands as Brooke guided *Verne*'s spherical white shape through the narrow underwater trench. As the robot sank between two towering rock faces, his high-definition video view went black. But Brooke's virtual display of the trench remained clear, part of thousands of square metres of the ocean floor previously mapped and stored in *Verne*'s memory.

Brooke began a steady roll to take *Verne* out of the ravine and on to the flat section of seabed where the scuba tanks were situated, when the robot veered suddenly to one side, grinding hard against the rock face before flipping on to his back.

'What's going on!' J.P. was on the radio net in a flash.

'I don't know! He just flipped out.'

'Can you move him?'

Brooke triggered full throttle, but *Verne* hardly budged at all. 'I think he's caught on something.'

'It'll be lobster netting.' Salty had come down from the bridge. 'They drift in the currents and get torn up around the rocks.'

'Damn it, Brooke!' J.P. smashed down his fist on the

cabin console. His face was bright red. 'For once, couldn't you have just done what you were told?'

Brooke pulled off the headset and glove and looked down at the deck. This time, she had nothing to say. Jackson could see she felt terrible. It didn't matter that Brooke was one of the most confident people Jackson had ever met; it was the second time in a week she'd let her father down, and he could see she was angry with herself.

Jackson followed her as she walked towards the front of the boat and opened the door to the hold. 'It wasn't your fault,' he said, not entirely confident he believed what he was saying.

'He's right, and you know it,' Brooke replied in frustration, searching hurriedly through several boxes and bags. 'I should have done what he asked, but I had to go and try somethin' fancy.'

'What are you doing now?' asked Jackson.

'Here they are!' she said, pulling a large blue-and-black triangle-shaped object from what looked like a waterproof pack, followed by a long knife in a rubber sheath. 'It's a mono-fin! Don't breath a word of this to Pops. By the time he realizes I'm in the water, I'll have freed *Verne* and be on my way back.'

A dumbfounded Jackson followed Brooke on to the deck as she turned away from the cabin and moved to the bow, out of sight of her father and Salty.

'This is a really bad idea, Brooke.'

'I can fix this, Jackson.' She smiled up at him from the deck on which she sat, clipping a weight belt round her waist and slipping a diving mask on to her forehead. 'I'll be back in a few minutes. If Dad asks, tell him I'm below deck. Now help me get this on.'

Brooke was holding what looked like the bottom section of a mermaid's costume. She slid one foot into the top of the carbon-fibre mono-fin and then leaned on Jackson while she slid in her other foot. She strapped the knife to her ankle, pulled her face mask down over her eyes and sat on the handrail that ran the length of the boat.

'See you in a jiffy!' Brooke said, and then promptly dropped backwards into the water.

Several hundred metres away from *The Oceanaut*, a dark-grey shape moved through the water at a speed few sea creatures could match. Like the spherical robot, whose whirling ripples had attracted the fish in the first place, it was able to adjust its course precisely. A series of subtle adjustments to its own control surfaces – smooth, rigid, pectoral fins – saw it navigate its deadly way with increasing purpose.

If Jackson hadn't been focusing quite so intently on the screen of his tablet PC, in an attempt to make out what *Verne* was snagged on, he might have seen his first Great White Shark. Its streamlined six-metre body glided diagonally underneath the boat and began to circle.

Salty spotted it immediately, taking his cap off and using it to wipe the sweat from his forehead.

'Well, would ya look at him! Ain't he a grand fella?'

'Who is?' Jackson looked up from the PC, confused.

'That old Great White,' Salty replied, not looking away from the waves.

Jackson froze. 'Do you mean *shark*?' He ran to the side of the boat and looked down into the water.

'They're very common in this part of the Atlantic,' J.P. said calmly, checking the monitors for signs of the animal. 'Get Brooke. She won't want to miss this.'

Jackson could hardly form the words. 'She's in the water!' he croaked.

All three men turned and looked at Jackson.

'How can she be?' said J.P. 'She's in the hold!'

'She was worried she'd let you down. She went down there to fetch her swimming fin. I tried to stop her, but she was over the side before I had time to say anything.'

'You idiot!' bellowed J.P.

Just then there was a deep thud against the hull of the boat and Jackson saw the dark outline of the shark hugging the side of *The Oceanaut* as it cruised slowly past.

'That's good news. At least it's us he's sizing up,' said Salty.

'Get me a tank, Salty,' J.P. shouted as he made for the hold at the other end of the boat. 'I'm going in after her!'

'You'll do no such thing!' ordered the old man, the eyes

in his weathered face tightening into a piercing stare. 'I'm the captain of this ship and you'll do as I say. Now quit running up and down like a puppy dog. Sharky seems pretty taken with *The Oceanaut*. For now, chances are he don't even know she's down there.'

'I hope you're right. I figure she's got about forty minutes on a tank. As long as she's spotted him, she'll make for one of the caves and sit it out.'

'She didn't take a tank,' whispered Jackson.

'No! Don't tell me she's free diving!' J.P.'s expression turned to horror.

'She didn't take anything but a big fin and a weight belt.'

'In a few minutes, she's going to have to come up for air!' said J.P.

Jackson felt sick.

Brooke had seen the Great White. She'd noticed the ominous outline of the huge fish within the first few seconds of her dive, its massive body blocking the sunlight as it glided overhead. The shock had made her gasp, and she'd had to fight to keep control of the air that wanted to rush out through her nose.

Free diving was the art of swimming underwater on a single breath. Brooke had learned the technique during summer breaks on Martha's Vineyard from the free divers who sometimes congregated on the island for competitions. She marvelled at their ability to stay submerged, sometimes for as long as ten minutes, on a single lungful of air. The technique required her to draw big slow breaths on the surface to lower her heart rate and expand her lungs. Once she was underwater, it was important she remain calm and composed as the faster her heart pumped, the more precious oxygen it would suck from her blood.

Seeing the six-metre shark hadn't done much for Brooke's composure, however. She had considered turning back to the boat, but something told her to continue her descent towards *Verne*, where she could turn and get a fix on the shark.

It became immediately clear that *Verne* was snagged on a flattened section of lobster netting. Part of a nylon rope, which was tangled round a sharp outcrop of rock, had been sucked into two of the robot's propeller shafts and he was stuck fast. Brooke swam quickly behind *Verne*, wedging herself in a gap in the rock before looking back up at the keel of *The Oceanaut* hovering like a big grey cloud above her. The shark dropped in and out of view in the shadows of the boat as it cruised a wide arc around it.

Brooke guessed that attempting to free *Verne* would take a good minute or so and might end up signalling her position to the Great White. She focused hard on trying to keep calm and giving her brain time to sort through the options. Swim now, while she still had all her strength, and try and beat the 30 kilometres per hour fish to the boat. Or sit tight and hope that he'd swim away in the two or so minutes she could remain down here.

Neither filled her with much hope.

Jackson caught his breath. His vigil at the monitors, while J.P. and Salty had been arguing about whether to dive in after Brooke, had paid off. 'It's Brooke! She's signalling to us.'

Brooke was clearly visible on the centre screen. She had squashed most of her body into a small crevice on the undersea rock face and was glaring, wide-eyed, into the camera. On close inspection, Jackson could make out a small yellow pipe coming from behind the camera and snaking its way into the side of her mouth.

'Well, I'll be damned,' said Salty. 'She's suckin' air outta that contraption a yours!'

'She must be using the tank that feeds the Oxy-Fuel combustion chamber. It's a small cylinder, filled with pure oxygen, that *Verne* uses as a kind of turbo charger! It should buy her some more time, but not much – the tank is tiny,' said J.P.

'How much oxygen does it hold?' asked Jackson.

'Three litres exactly,' the professor replied.

'She'll suck in . . . I'm guessing 1,800 millilitres per breath? Hold it in for, say, three minutes . . . after all, even for a free diver, this is a high stress situation. So, 600 millilitres a minute. Factor in a percentage of oxygen loss, because that pipe's not a perfect delivery mechanism . . . what, twenty per cent?'

Jackson looked up at the others. 'I'd suggest she has five minutes' breathing time. Roughly,' he concluded.

'I'll be darned,' said Salty. 'He *is* a computer.'

'That's all great,' said J.P. 'But unless we figure out a way of luring that shark away from the area, your maths isn't going to do her much good.'

The two older men started talking hurriedly through suggestions for leading the shark away, but Jackson wasn't listening. He had his own idea.

It was a safe bet that the notion of flying *Tug* and *Punk* out to the boat wouldn't be one that J.P. would agree to. But as Jackson remotely triggered the robots' flash start-up sequences, he was confident that his plan stood at least as much chance of success as the pretend seal J.P. was forcing a reluctant Salty to construct out of a bright orange buoy and strips of an old brown towel.

Jackson sent a simple text message: 'U ERE TP SPD'. A moment after receiving it, *Punk* and *Tug* obeyed, flying at top speed in tight formation barely half a metre above the sea's surface towards the GPS coordinates of the phone where the message was sent from. Jackson calculated that a straight-line, flat-out run would take them about five minutes. It was going to be tight.

Until they arrived, Jackson would dedicate himself to Project Towelling Seal. He looked over to see J.P. fumbling with a length of thin metal rope he had wound round the tubular towel-covered buoy. The professor, who had dedicated his life to the design and construction of robots, was so distracted with worry that he was all fingers and thumbs.

Salty unceremoniously barged J.P. out of the way and proceeded to tie a hangman's knot with the wire, then secured the creation to a sturdy-looking fishing rod.

Not quite sure what else to do, now that Salty had taken over from his efforts on the towelling seal, J.P. explained his plan to Jackson. 'Research into attacks by this species of shark on humans suggests they attack swimmers, which they mistake for seals. If we can cast my seal far enough out and reel it in at the correct speed, we might stand a chance of hooking him. If Salty's right, and he's a two-tonner, we'll not be able to land him. But with a hook in him, we'll know where he is and might be able to slow him down if we all get behind it! That should give me the time I need to swim down to Brooke and signal.'

'Are you sure you need to go into the water too?'

'We know she can't see much down there. It's the only way I can signal to Brooke when it's safe to surface.'

Jackson looked at the pretend seal now dangling over the edge of the boat. It turned slowly; a large steel hook glinted in the sunlight. He glanced at his mobile phone – seven minutes and counting.

Salty stood astride the base of the large metal fishing rod that sat in a holder, screwed to the deck by ten centimetre-wide nuts. It was an impressive set-up, but as Jackson took position alongside the old fisherman, he wondered if the hardware was up to the job. With his large strong hands Salty pushed the rod forward and then pulled it back as far as the eleven-metre metal pole would flex, letting it whip forward and catapult the bizarre makeshift mammal out to sea.

It was an impressive cast. The bait splashed down at least thirty metres in the opposite direction to Brooke. Salty started to wind in the line, the wrinkly, sun-baked skin on his arms stretching over rippling muscles as he frantically turned the handle on the rod's massive, industrial-strength reel.

The shark continued its patrol. It hadn't detected the scent of anything, and had found little of interest beyond the subtle vibrations that had brought it here, save for the large white mass around which it was circling. The shark didn't know what it was, or why it had come to rest in this place. And, even after millions of years of evolution, the great fish had no way of knowing that it was a boat, with people on board who found the fish's presence utterly terrifying. All that drove this example of the ocean's most efficient killing machine was a primeval instinct that something edible was near.

Then something changed – a rhythm in the waves and

a current that hadn't been there before. An irregular and turbulent flick-flack on the surface of the water that signalled something sizeable and possibly palatable.

Jackson and the rest of the crew of *The Oceanaut* saw the Great White's pectoral fin cresting the surf for the first time since the huge animal's arrival. It circled again but, this time, its radius pointed towards the dummy seal and not *The Oceanaut*. Then it vanished.

'Brace yourselves, lads, he's coming in, full steam,' cried Salty.

Jackson was scared now. He gripped his part of the rod and pushed his feet hard down into his trainers. He didn't have to worry for long. The shark appeared like a rocket, rising vertically from below the pathetic pretend prey, water frothing around its gills like steam on a launch pad. Jackson saw what he thought was the glint of the steel hook before everything disappeared in a puff of spray. Salty let go of the reel, which became a crazed Catherine wheel until he slammed down the brake switch. The moment the brake bit into the steel line, *The Oceanaut* lunged towards its starboard side. Boxes, bags, robot battery packs, and almost J.P. himself, slid into the water as the monstrous animal, bait in mouth, attempted to swim away.

'For God's sake! What are you doing?' yelled J.P.

'Leave the fishing to me, Prof,' shouted Salty, anchoring the rod with one bulging bicep. 'Your poor excuse for dinner ain't gonna pass the taste test. I needs to keep it sprightly, or he'll lose interest! Wait till he got the hook, then we can decide what we do next.'

'How d'you know he's not hooked yet?' asked Jackson.

'You just know!'

'Well, make sure you don't keep it to yourself,' said J.P., who was still having trouble standing on the listing deck. He was now fully suited up for the rescue mission with wetsuit, face mask, tank and regulator. Jackson also noted he had the biggest knife he'd ever seen strapped to the outside of his leg. Jackson knew the professor was a man of many talents, but he had difficulty imagining him in the role of shark fighter.

'There! Can you feel him? Now he's hooked!' shouted Salty.

Jackson quickly lent his support to the old man's efforts to control the frenzied yanks of a tonne of muscle on the line.

Suddenly the line went slack and Salty shouted to J.P. to watch the line.

'He's coming about!' yelled Salty. 'If he decides he wants to show us how strong he is, and you're in the way of that line, it'll slice you in two!'

'If he goes anywhere north of us, shout,' called J.P. 'That'll be my chance to go for Brooke!'

Salty let out a grumble, which wasn't too far removed from the sound the engines of *The Oceanaut* made when they were first fired up. He still didn't agree with J.P.'s plan to go in after his daughter but there wasn't much else he could do either.

With the line still slack, the Great White appeared beside the boat, drifting slowly past the starboard side. It was the first time that Jackson could take in the scale of the animal. It was more than half the length of *The Oceanaut*. And it was so close he could smell it, a jagged stench of stale meat that stuck in his nostrils. The shark was under the boat now, moving diagonally, and Salty's reel was whirling again.

'I'm going in!' J.P. shouted, and a moment later he dropped below the stern of the boat.

Brooke had been observing the effects of her father and the crew on their uninvited guest. She had watched as something vaguely resembling her rolled-up beach towel had landed in the water before becoming shark bait. She couldn't see the fishing line as parts of her diving mask were now steamed up, but she got the general idea. Pound for pound, the engineer in her didn't rate *The Oceanaut*'s chances of winning if it came to a tug of war between the boat and the shark.

Still trapped in the crevice of the underwater rock face, Brooke clutched *Verne* to her, having cut away most of the nylon fishing net. She thought how, if she ever got out of this mess alive, she would advise her father on a new design for a protective fender that could be retro-fitted round all of *Verne*'s propellers. Brooke had kind of left her dad to fend for himself on the *Verne* project. She rarely helped him out at all these days; she was too much into her own stuff. No two ways about it, she was a bad daughter.

Note to self, thought Brooke. *Apologize to Dad for shark incident. Help Dad with his robots. Tell Dad his sports car was in fact washed out to sea.*

Just when Brooke thought she couldn't feel any more guilty, she spotted the unmistakable shape of her father in a wetsuit leaving the safety of *The Oceanaut*.

And, unless this was some horrible nightmare, she could also make out the outline of the shark, turning towards him in the distance.

CHAPTER 14

The sensation of forcibly regurgitating a seal was a new one for the shark.

As the huge animal hurtled downwards and the reel ran out of line, the force jerked the mock bait and hook clean out of its stomach.

'He's loose, damn it!' shouted Salty, the metal rod whipping back as all the tension went from it.

The professor felt a surge of fear race through his body. He'd been scared when he had entered the water, but this was different. It was as if his body knew something he didn't. In any other circumstances he would have stopped and turned round to confirm what his senses were telling him, that a shark was following him. But his daughter was down there and he simply had to get to her.

There are between seventy and a hundred recorded shark attacks a year, he told himself as he swam desperately downwards. *And, of those, an average of eight are considered fatal. The odds are in my favour,* he thought. *Keep swimming.*

Brooke saw things differently. As her father finally

reached her, the shark was less than a few metres behind him, jaws agape and closing at terrific speed. She grabbed the straps on J.P.'s back and used them to heave him into the space behind *Verne*. With one quick thrust of its tail, the shark collided with the white robot, its gaping jaws clamping down on it like a steam press, ripping it from in front of J.P. and Brooke.

With a fast flurry of bites and twists, the shark soon worked out that the ball of syntactic foam and complex alloys wouldn't make for easy digesting and let *Verne* fall from its mouth. It then turned into a sweeping arc that it intended would bring it back to the rock face with enough momentum to make it into the cave.

Salty was familiar with the English family's penchant for exotic machinery. Since J.P. had been a child, let alone Brooke, Salty had been roped in to help test or retrieve all manner of modified vehicles designed for land, sea and air. Even so, the two contraptions that had just arrived above *The Oceanaut* were very strange indeed.

'At the risk of askin' a silly question: are those two waterproof?'

'Not exactly,' Jackson replied. As he continued to speak, he sent a text message to the two robots – 'HLDNG PTTRN' – ordering them to stay overhead. 'But they were designed to operate in the vacuum of space, so all their important bits should be sealed.'

'What about their unimportant bits?' ventured Matty.

'It's a little late to worry about that now. I guess we're about to find out.'

With the robots in a steady cruise above the boat, Jackson watched the live feed from *Verne* through the doorway of the cabin as the robot came to rest upside down on the seabed. Despite his encounter with the shark, *Verne*'s vital statistics, represented by a series of numbers down the side of the screen, showed he was still functioning fine. Jackson quickly copied the first two lines of numbers into his phone and prepared to send them as a text message to *Punk* and *Tug*.

To Jackson, at least, his plan was simple. The robots' new Artificial Intelligence programming, which had brought them safely to the boat, could be used to guide them both to *Verne* – and therefore within very close proximity to Brooke and her father. And the shark. Jackson could use their infrared scanners to identify the shark's heat signal and seek it out. He'd seen both robots do enough damage on land to know that, unlike *Verne*, they were a match for a shark. With *Punk* and *Tug* thinking for themselves, Jackson would be free to control *Verne*, via the goggles and control glove which Brooke had left behind.

He sent the message containing *Verne*'s precise location on the sea floor:

Instantly, *Tug* broke formation and nose-dived into the water. *Punk*, however, continued to fly in circles around the boat.

Jackson's handset pulsed with warmth. He glanced down and saw an emoticon on its screen surface. It was from *Punk*: (o_<)

The robot was flinching. He was telling Jackson, through his digital sign language, that he was too scared to follow *Tug* into the water. Jackson would have laughed, if the situation weren't so dire. He would have to deal with him in a minute – for now it was crucial to get *Tug* to the seabed.

Tug registered the experience of flying in a liquid, for his first time, in the only way he knew how, as an extreme and instant change in weather pressure and ambient temperature.

For a few seconds he overcompensated and, instead of subtly adjusting his course towards *Verne*'s location, the stunted flaps and ducts of fast-moving air at the rear of his triangular body that provided directional control pushed too hard against the water, causing him to spiral. But within a few seconds *Tug* had computed the important new variables of his underwater environment, the weight of the water molecules and the increased drag they caused on his sleek body.

'TGT LRGST HEAT SIG,' Jackson texted *Tug*.

'B(~_^)D,' replied the robot, his sensitive thermal-imaging system scanning the water ahead of him.

Tug's view of the sea floor instantly changed. The aquamarine blue, shot through with shafts of sparkling white light, was replaced by almost total blackout. Jackson watched the same view on his handset, but it was nowhere near as clear as it would have been on the surface, as the salt and silt in the water were absorbing much of the red light from *Tug*'s emitter. But, as *Tug* was nearing *Verne*'s position, his tracking software locked on to the outlines of three faint shapes, automatically drawing a box round each.

Jackson inspected the grainy images closely and realized that the two smallest shapes at the bottom of *Tug*'s feed represented the heads of Brooke and J.P. who were sharing the professor's oxygen feed in the mouth of the cave. But the luminous splotch of yellow and red above them belonged to something much bigger. It was the Great White. Following his orders, *Tug* fixed on the large warm mass of the shark.

'SHNT TRGT.'

Almost as soon as Jackson's command arrived, *Tug*'s SHUNT thruster was spooling up. A potent mix of combustible fuel and gases exploded within a blast-proof chamber inside the chisel-shaped machine. The high-tensile steel and woven Kevlar inner-casing, which gave

Tug's nose the strength of a battering ram, drove home the force of his powerful surge through the water. But the blow on the Great White was only glancing. The shark, an agile predator, as practised in avoiding attacks as it was at delivering them, rolled to avoid the full force of the power punch.

With nothing to absorb the energy of his charge, *Tug* carried straight on, smashing into a jagged cluster of rock and coral. His logic engine instantly computed the need to reverse, but his relatively weak reverse thrusters were no match for the tight grip of the rocky fissure into which he had wedged himself.

On the deck of *The Oceanaut*, Jackson knew that only *Punk* could help now.

'FLLW TG,' he ordered.

'FLLW HM USLF,' replied *Punk*.

Jackson had attempted every form of persuasion he could think of, but couldn't get past *Punk*'s prudent personality, the personality he himself had created. Jackson had programmed *Punk* to be cautious of anything that might threaten his optimum functioning and, as he had said several times in the last minute, 'PNK DNT SWM'.

With *Tug* immobilized, the only course of action left to Jackson was to take control himself. Jackson typed 'I HV CNTRL' into his mobile-phone keypad and sent it straight to *Punk*.

Punk faltered in the air for a moment, before Jackson

got the measure of the microscopic accelerometer and digital compass components of his handset, then threw the spiked robot down towards the ocean.

A gestural input later and *Punk*'s three rotor blades snapped inside his metal body, milliseconds before he entered the water.

The shark had completed another one of its quick circuits round the rocks where Brooke and J.P. were hiding. And now it was gathering speed for another run at the cave. It closed at a frightening pace, driven by its primitive impulse to feed, and perhaps, thought Brooke, after meeting *Tug*, a dose of self-preservation.

This time, she thought, there was little chance that she and her father would survive.

In the split second before the shark smashed into the cave, Brooke was sure she could make out surprise in his small black eyes. She didn't see *Punk* shooting downwards through the water, or three of his sharp spines piercing the smooth, grey skin and thin layer of blubber that covered the shark's back. But she couldn't miss the pulse of electric-blue light that engulfed the creature as Jackson remotely triggered the robot's cattle-prod function. The shark's enormous body radiated with a blue-and-white glow. It still smashed into the wall of rock with crushing force, but the stunned animal was too dazed to chase the two swimmers who dived out of its way and started to swim for the surface.

A few moments later an exhausted Brooke and J.P.

were hauled on to the deck of *The Oceanaut* by Jackson, Matty and Salty.

'You are seriously grounded, young lady!' said J.P., through quick gulps for breath, hugging his daughter tightly and kissing her soaked head. 'And as for you, Farley,' he gasped. 'Great job!'

'Thank you, sir,' said Jackson, looking up from his phone.

'The robots!' Brooke wheezed. 'Are they going to be OK?'

'I'm not sure,' said Jackson.

Jackson crouched by Brooke and shared the view from his handset. It was hard to determine exactly what was going on, as thick plumes of silt clouded the picture, but the serrated triangular blades that were the Great White's teeth flashed repeatedly across the screen, as the huge fish nudged *Punk* along the seabed like a football.

'*Punk*'s already several hundred metres north-east of us,' said Jackson, rushing over to the remote glove and goggles that lay on the decking. '*Verne* is still functional; there's a small chance I can use him to recover *Punk*.'

'Don't bother,' said Salty. 'The shark's takin' him to Swallow Hole. You'd best dig your other contraption out while you've got the chance.'

The crew watched the feed from *Punk* for several minutes longer, while Jackson attempted to use *Verne*'s grapplers to drag *Tug* out of his hole.

The last thing *Punk* transmitted before he disconnected was a tumbling view of rock followed by pitch black.

It was dusk when *The Oceanaut* docked in the marina at Oak Bluffs.

It was immediately obvious to the exhausted crew that something unusual was happening because the quays were empty of the usual tourists and old fishermen paying the setting sun their last respects. It seemed everyone on the island was packed inside the restaurants. What was going on?

Brooke and Jackson were first off the boat and had to stand on tables outside a cafe in order to look over the heads of people packed inside to see what all the fuss was about.

There, in the centre of a room crammed to bursting with the thunderstruck spectators, was a large flatscreen. The news channel's headline was crystal clear:

MIT's Nuclear Reactor Attacked!

CHAPTER 15

Goulman had made it out of Boston on one of the first flights and had arrived at the Englishs' house on the island in time for breakfast.

Brooke's mother made bacon and pancakes for everyone during the vigil round the television. Every news channel was covering what they were calling a terrorist attack on the university's reactor. For most of the morning, reporters and news anchors had focused on footage of a large and obvious circular hole, which had been cut into the front door of the reactor building. But, by early afternoon, all the attention was on grainy images released by the authorities, which had reportedly revealed a similar round hole in the wall of the reactor compartment itself.

The city of Boston had been declared a nuclear disaster zone and helicopter shots showed traffic jamming up every road that led out of the city, every footbridge and pavement clogged up by people – even the Charles River had been turned into an expressway, chock-full of boats ferrying people out of the city.

After spending all morning and most of the afternoon glued to the television, Brooke and Jackson had decided to walk into town for some fresh air and dinner at Brooke's favourite diner.

'It was bound to happen,' drawled the waitress, laying a plate in front of Jackson that contained the biggest burger he had ever seen. 'The weird thing, as I sees it, is that they left the fuel rods!'

Jackson thought it sounded weird to hear such scientific words as 'fuel rods' said in the old lady's strong Boston accent – but the news channels and newspapers had used so much nuclear power-related phraseology so often during the course of the day that they were on the lips of everyone on the island.

'Mmm, gimme some of that!' said Brooke, leaning over the table and grabbing Jackson's burger with both hands before taking a big bite.

'You could have bought your own, you know. No one forced you to go with the salad.'

'Girl's gotta watch her figure!' she mumbled through a mouthful of Jackson's burger.

'Seems like a guy's gotta watch his burger!' Jackson retaliated. 'She's right, though – the waitress, that is – it is strange that someone would go to all the trouble of drilling a hole in a reactor wall, but not steal the most precious thing in there.'

'They were spooked. That's what the news guy said.'

'Yeah, but by what?' Jackson pointed at the open newspaper in front of him. 'Look, it says here that all the security cameras in the reactor and neighbouring vicinity were taken out by the attackers.'

'And?' Brooke had seized the opportunity to snag another mouthful of Jackson's burger as he focused on the newspaper.

'They have no evidence of anyone being spooked. They're clutching at straws because they can't explain why someone would enter a reactor and leave everything alone.'

'Chaos,' said Brooke, wiping mayonnaise from her chin.

'What do you mean, *chaos*?' asked Jackson.

'Isn't that what all terrorism is about? Creating panic and fear! The city of Boston has virtually shut down. Even people who live and work miles outside the designated danger zone have left the city in droves.'

'A truck bomb I would understand, if panic and confusion were the aim of the exercise,' said Jackson. 'But why the precision hole? It says here that the reactor wall was ninety-eight-centimetre-thick steel-reinforced concrete that would have required an industrial-strength drilling machine to get through it. What kind of terrorists have that technology at their disposal?'

'A robot could do that.' Brooke stopped eating, suddenly interested in the debate. 'A drilling platform like they use for oil and gas exploration. Dad used to design them.' Then she checked herself. 'But they're too big. It's unlikely someone could roll up with one of those babies without anyone seeing it.'

'What about a robot swarm?' asked Jackson excitedly.

Brooke's forehead creased. 'For someone who walked out of Singer's lecture, you seem to have been inspired by an awful lot of his ideas!'

Jackson ignored her. 'Why not?'

'Well, if you're right, and there's a terrorist group with that kind of tech, we're in a lot of trouble. If next time they decide to take the fuel rods, they could make a portable radioactive device –'

'A dirty bomb?' Jackson interrupted.

'Yep! One they could set off anywhere in America.'

It was a nightmare scenario: even a small amount of explosive could be used to blow radioactive material into thousands of tiny pieces, scattering deadly irradiated debris around a populated area.

'What are the chances someone could have developed a robot swarm?'

'Ask Goulman,' said Brooke, looking up at her father's assistant as he walked into the diner.

'Dad? In custody?' Brooke gasped 'How can he be?'

'The sheriff just turned up at the house,' Goulman said gravely, ushering the two of them into her father's jeep. 'He had two FBI agents with him. They took him away.'

'Sheriff Townsend?' Brooke asked, dumfounded.

'Yes. The agents said they think the reactor was attacked by a drilling robot.'

Jackson and Brooke stared at each other, stupefied.

'As you know, Brooke, J.P. used to work on robots like that and his name came up in connection with damaging university property.'

'Damaging university property?' Brooke said stonily. Then her eyes widened as she seemed to make a connection. 'Not the dorm fire case?'

'Yes,' said Goulman. 'They think he might have a grudge.'

'You have to be kidding!' Brooke looked on the verge of tears. 'But . . . but that was my fault – and *Fist* and I saved lives!'

'You've seen the news,' Goulman continued as he drove. 'The police are desperate to find someone responsible for all this. Right now, Brooke, they're questioning your father.'

'Where have they taken him?' Brooke demanded.

'He's being questioned at the sheriff's office,' said Goulman.

'Put your foot down and get me there now!' Brooke insisted. She pulled her phone out of her pocket and punched in some numbers. 'Sheriff Townsend, please,' she said through gritted teeth. 'Yes, in the Vineyard Haven police office . . .'

As Brooke bawled at someone in the sheriff's office

who had obviously made the mistake of not perceiving her need for urgency, Jackson edged forward towards Goulman.

'You've done some work on swarm robotics, right?' he asked him quietly.

'What?' said Goulman, taken aback by Jackson's question.

'You made some swarm robot prototypes?'

'What has that got to do with anything, Jackson?' Goulman said, punching the words out. He frowned at Jackson for a moment before turning his attention back to the road, then added, 'I'm sorry. It's just that with everything that's going on, I'd rather focus on J.P.'

'I just wondered . . .' Jackson let his sentence drift away. 'It doesn't matter.'

Perhaps this wasn't the right time to test his theory, thought Jackson. Things were, after all, pretty bad for Brooke and Goulman right now. Plus he didn't want to get Brooke into any more trouble by raising Goulman's suspicions about why he was asking. But as the jeep raced along the causeway, he noticed Goulman in the mirror, watching him.

Tokyo, Japan. 9 p.m.

'Miss Kojima, is there any truth in the reports that you and your brother plan to launch a pop career if you win next week's competition?'

Miss Kojima looked at the journalist who had just asked the question. She was sure that every time the ten-year-old professional gamer and her brother agreed to do an interview, the questions they were asked got dumber.

As finalists in the Japan Cyber Olympics, the toughest and most prestigious computing-gaming competition in all of East Asia, this press conference was unavoidable.

Miss Kojima looked at the slightly balding, moustached Japanese TV reporter who had asked the question, and the mass of faces around him that waited to ask more. She had a great answer lined up – one that involved her leaping to her feet in front of all the cameras and proving how stupid the question was by demonstrating just how badly she could sing the Japanese translation of 'Hit Me Baby One More Time' by Britney Spears. Just as well for everyone, her father answered the question for her.

'No,' said Mr Kojima, his stony expression unmoving. 'These rumours are just silly. Next question.'

It was as if a piece of meat had been thrown into a pool of piranhas – questions snapped up at the stage on which the twins and their father sat with an entourage that included press consultants, fashion stylists, brand managers, a nutritionist and two personal trainers.

'Have you planned your competition tactics?'

'Is it true you're going to buy an island if you win the tournament?'

'Which of the other teams do you fear most?

'What if you lose?'

'How's the movie coming along?'

'How many Ferraris do you own now?'

As her father selected which of the hundreds of questions he wanted to answer, Miss Kojima turned her attention to her smartphone. Her father had had them practising so hard over the last few days for the forthcoming competition that she hadn't had time to check her emails. The first few were from journalists. More questions. *Unbelievable!* she thought. Then one from yesterday caught her attention.

Email from: Jackson Farley

While her father refused to confirm either way that the twins had or hadn't done a deal with Nike, she opened the email and read its contents. She then slid the phone along the table, until it was under her brother's nose.

Master Kojima had been slouched, listening to music on his personalized brand of gaming headphones, for the entire press conference. He lifted his shades on to his forehead and read the email on the phone.

Both twins stood up at the same time, bowed to the audience of journalists, and then to their astonished father, before walking straight out of the room.

CHAPTER 16

Cambridge was on virtual lock-down for a week. The news had shown little else but soldiers in masks wearing special protective clothing while manning roadblocks. Brooke and Jackson had stayed on Martha's Vineyard, where J.P. remained in custody, his daughter allowed an hour a day to visit him.

With the breach to the nuclear reactor sealed and Cambridge's hot-zone status finally removed, J.P. was moved to a bigger police facility on the mainland, in Boston city.

Brooke and Jackson left the island too, Jackson returning to his dorm, and Brooke opting to sleep in the lab. J.P.'s lab had been ransacked by FBI investigators, every inch of it turned upside down. All the robots had been taken away for examination, but when police found no trace of the reactor building's dust or radioactivity on them, J.P.'s lawyer had filed a court order demanding that they be returned. The robots were back in their pens now and Brooke had pulled her couch up and slept beside them ever since, like a faithful guard dog.

Jackson knew she felt responsible. From what he could gather, one of the pieces of evidence that was keeping J.P. in custody was his previous record of criminal damage to university property. He had taken the blame for the university dorm fire in which Brooke had unwittingly caused damage in her rescue attempt, to protect his daughter. And now, as far as Brooke was concerned, her father was behind bars for something she had done.

Brooke would have owned up to the whole thing if J.P.'s lawyer hadn't been around to advise her of the consequences of revisiting the million-dollar lawsuit. His advice was that she be patient – a quality that didn't come naturally to Brooke.

When Jackson wasn't keeping Brooke company, he spent most of his time in his dorm room. With lectures cancelled for a couple of weeks, only about half of the students had returned to Simmons Hall and the building was more peaceful than usual – less music vibrating through the walls from the other rooms and fewer cries from the sports fields. He'd consciously decided to stop thinking about his mother and real father and concentrate his efforts on trying to get to the bottom of the nuclear reactor mystery to help J.P. The mathematics course papers he needed to work through for MIT didn't get in the way of his research into what had happened

– he always found number-crunching to be a great way of focusing his mind.

Jackson allowed his brain to juggle all the variables involved with the reactor attack – the fact that no one saw anything, the lack of any evidence on the CCTV, the size of the holes. Whatever he read about the attack, the swarm robot theory he'd mentioned to Brooke in the diner seemed to fit. And whatever newspaper images and TV news footage he saw of the holes in the door and reactor, the cartoon-like pictures from Singer's lecture came back to him.

It was regrettable for J.P., Jackson decided, that his fortunes had been made in the oil industry. His revolutionary ideas for automated drill-bots that could seek out pockets of valuable black gold were the main reason his lawyer had, as yet, failed to quash the preposterous allegations against him. The fact he had no oil-drilling robotics in his laboratory when the FBI searched it was considered evidence that the machines used on the reactor had been hidden. And his alibi, namely that he was out on the boat during the attack, with no less than four witnesses, including Jackson, was countered by the Feds' assertion that he didn't need to be at the scene of the attack because his drilling robots could have been autonomous.

The good news was that he hadn't been charged yet and was only *helping police with their enquiries.* According to the English family lawyer, it was likely that J.P. would be released any day soon.

That just left the question of who actually had carried out the attack. The FBI had made up their mind, but Jackson was determined to prove them wrong. He focused, as he had so many times, on the shape of the hole. He had several images of it that he'd kept from the newspapers, the more detailed of which showed that the edge of the hole undulated with curved teeth all around. Jackson visualized the collection of tiny robots that Singer spoke about, joined together to form different shapes. What if Singer's swarm bots weren't small cubes as his artist's impression had shown – what if they were spherical instead? A ring of spherical robots would fit the shape of the reactor hole perfectly.

Was that what had attacked the reactor? he thought. *A ring of drill-bots each sharing the task of chewing their way through the one-metre-thick reactor wall?*

And what about the question of who was behind them? Terrorists? A master criminal? Someone who'd known Lear? Since Singer had mentioned him in the context of swarm robotics, Jackson couldn't help feeling that the dead man's presence kept cropping up.

Jackson salvaged the screwed-up piece of newspaper given to him by Goulman and re-read the diamond robbery article.

He had stared at the photograph of the diamond mine

guards holding their stomachs and checked it against the horrible images he carried in his head of men squirming with the effects of Bass Bombs he himself had detonated while flying MeX machines for Lear. Had someone taken up Lear's reins at MeX?

But if this diamond heist was their work, then how did it relate to an attack on a reactor, just a few hundred metres from where he was sitting?

Jackson pulled up every article he could find on the Internet relating to the events surrounding Lear's disappearance. Most intriguing were the blogs and forums that featured supposed sightings of Lear himself, his boats and, most ridiculously, a luxury motorhome – in Paraguay, Argentina and Brazil.

Jackson felt sick as he let surface the one thought he'd been trying to squash: *What if it was Lear himself?* Ignoring every sensible bone in his body that was telling him this was just the old paranoia, Jackson sketched out a scenario in his head. *Suppose Lear had staged his own death*, he thought. Most official reports seemed to agree that his yacht had vanished off the coast of Spain, but the majority of unofficial sightings after that, the ones Jackson had found on the Internet, suggested the possibility that Lear had surfaced again in South America. Was it so preposterous that Lear's death was a fake and that he'd been living ever since in South America? A rich, dead man with a talent for designing robots had all the time and resources required to finish development of a miniature robotic swarm. And what better way for a criminal to put them to the test than with a daring diamond heist?

In Jackson's opinion, it was possible that Lear's swarm was behind a South American diamond heist and a North American reactor attack. What Jackson couldn't understand was the connection between the two.

But he knew someone who might.

Atticus79 had greeted Jackson's knock with a beaming smile. Jackson loved that about the skinny geologist at the end of his corridor: he was always so pleased to see him.

Setting foot inside Atticus79's dorm room was like venturing into a cave – rocks sparkled from floor to ceiling and the light from his window hit hundreds of crystal formations, some the size of melons, which he used for bookends, doorstops and paperweights, shattering the sunlight into a million colourful shards.

'Please come and sit down,' said Atticus79, waving Jackson inside. 'Chess?'

'Sit where?' said Jackson, unable to see a single place among the shallow wooden boxes of rock samples, maps and books that encrusted the cave floor.

'Excuse the mess,' Atticus79 said, snapping cases shut and shifting piles of books to reveal a beanbag. 'I'm using all this madness on campus to get ahead in my studies.

What about that? A terrorist attack on our university! I know a few students who thought they deserved an 'A', but getting their revenge with a dirty bomb? That's over-kill!' Atticus79 guffawed until his glasses almost fell off.

Jackson couldn't bring himself to even pretend to laugh along with Atticus79; things were still too messed up. Instead he got straight to the point of why he'd come here. 'Do you know anything about diamonds?'

If Atticus79 noticed the dramatic change in subject, he didn't show it. 'Diamond, from the ancient Greek *adámas*, meaning "proper" or "unalterable".' He pulled down a large heavy book from one of the shelves with the words *Manual of Mineralogy* stamped in gold on the cover. 'What do you want to know?'

'Just general stuff,' said Jackson. He actually had no idea what he was looking for exactly, just a hunch that Atticus79 might be able to give him some clue as to why, if it was Lear, he would be pulling off such an audacious heist and appearing in Jackson's life again.

'General stuff?' Atticus79 frowned.

Jackson thought on his feet; he did not want to rouse his friend's suspicion. 'Yeah. Brooke has asked me to research new materials,' he replied as nonchalantly as he could.

'Well, I know diamonds are used in some semiconductors because they conduct heat extremely well.'

'Really?'

'Yes. As silicon computer processors are becoming smaller and more powerful, they are becoming hotter. A diamond computer processor, on the other hand, doesn't get as hot and that makes it more efficient.'

Atticus79 leafed quickly through a few pages of the book and then gave it to Jackson.

'There. Look!' he said, stabbing at a page of graphs. 'Look at those heat coefficient figures for diamonds!' For once, Jackson wasn't interested in the maths; he was more interested in a diagram on the facing page of a big fat blue diamond with the words 'Largest irradiated diamond' written below it.

'What's an *irradiated diamond*?' asked Jackson.

'Diamond companies have been exposing diamonds to radiation for years to colour plain white diamonds.'

Plain white diamonds. Jackson remembered the words from the Brazilian newspaper article.

'They put the white diamonds in the reactor,' Atticus79 continued. 'And when they come out, they're a different colour, usually blue, then other colours like yellow or pink can be achieved by continuing the process.'

'Why turn a plain diamond blue?' Jackson asked.

Atticus79 laughed. 'Why do you think? To increase its value, of course!'

'How long does the process take?' Jackson asked.

'Just a few days,' replied Atticus79.

The jigsaw pieces in Jackson's mind suddenly began

to click together. Could Lear have come out of hiding to steal a shipment of white diamonds and then, using swarm technology, break into the nuclear reactor on Jackson's very doorstep to let the gemstones cook?

To anyone else that might have sounded like the paranoid worries of an overanxious teenager. But Jackson had dealt with Lear before and he knew he would be capable of something like this.

If it's true, and Lear is still alive, Jackson thought, *any day now, his swarm will be returning to the reactor to collect the diamonds.*

CHAPTER 17

Jackson peeled away from the traffic on his Cannondale Bad Boy and took a short cut to the Fire Proof building that would take him around a network of old warehouses. He wanted to get to the laboratory as quickly as possible and tell Brooke what he thought he might have pieced together.

As he entered the maze of alleyways, he noticed that another cyclist had turned in behind him, the whizz of the other bike's gears echoing between the walls of the buildings. When Jackson glanced round, he could only just see the shadowy figure of the cyclist as, unlike him, his headlights were not on.

Several turns later and the old paranoia was back, but, with his new theory about Lear, Jackson wasn't going to discount anything. There were enough intersecting alleyways in this part of Cambridge to send a cyclist anywhere in the city – so what were the chances that the guy behind was going to the exact same destination as Jackson?

Jackson decided to put him to the test. He threw a right, shaving the side of a second-hand car dealership, then another right, followed by a third, until he was back to where he'd started. Sure enough, as he headed away from the car lot, the figure of a man on a bike hovered behind him.

So, he thought, *I'm not going mad after all. Someone* is *following me!*

But who was it? One thing he knew for sure was that he wasn't going to wait around to find out. Jackson pressed down hard on the pedals and pushed the red button on his handlebars. He could feel the electric hub urging his back wheel forward, as a torrent of electrons gushed from the chemical reaction inside his bike frame. In four seconds he had gone from 30 kilometres an hour to 60. The next turn would bring him on to the main road and then he could really let rip.

Jackson leaned into the corner, which took him round the edge of a shady office block and . . . a dead end!

What had happened to the main road? Somewhere behind, he must have taken a wrong turn.

Jackson slammed on the bike's hydraulic brakes and a shuddering shockwave spread throughout the frame as it stopped, millimetres from a brick wall.

Jackson looked up in horror as his pursuer rounded the corner. Then he let out a huge sigh of relief – it was an MIT bike cop.

'Wow, am I pleased to see you, officer,' said Jackson, sweat dripping down the side of his face.

'Really?' said the police officer, raising an eyebrow and pulling a notebook from his breast pocket. 'Most speeding cyclists have the opposite reaction when they see me.'

'I'm sorry about that, sir.' Jackson pushed out his words between deep breaths. 'I thought you were someone else. Someone chasing me.'

The cop smiled. 'Lucky for you then, you're just getting a speeding ticket.'

Jackson watched the cop as he slowly scrawled notes on his pad. He asked where Jackson had been and where he was going. Jackson mentioned he was going to visit a friend but left it at that. But the police officer continued to ask the same questions, going over Jackson's plans for the evening, and questioning every detail. It was odd. As the officer continued to scribble, Jackson cast a glance over the man's bike. Not only did it not have any headlights, it didn't have the siren and police hazard lights like the other MIT police mountain bikes he'd seen. There was no waterproof battery-pack rack on the back – in fact, there was no rack there at all. And now that Jackson looked more closely, there was a lot about the bike that didn't seem to add up. Although the colour was right and it said 'Specialized' on the side, next to 'MIT Police', in Jackson's bike-geek opinion it wasn't a Specialized frame – the angle of the top tube was wrong and it was too thin to be aluminium, but was more like steel alloy tubing.

'Nice bike,' said Jackson.

'Thank you,' the cop replied, smiling.

'Full aluminium frame?'

'You bet!' replied the cop.

He didn't want to guess at the reason, but Jackson knew the cop was lying. And he also knew he needed to get out of the alleyway – fast.

Jackson pushed past the policeman, knocking the man's bike to the ground. He pressed the power button while he was still running and jumped on to his bike's seat, forcing his legs to power down on to the pedals. Jackson was already passing 30 kilometres an hour when he looked behind and saw the bogus police officer struggling to get moving – there was no way he was going to catch Jackson.

But focused on losing the fraudulent cop, Jackson failed to turn his eyes back to the road in time to see the black van that had pulled across, blocking his exit.

The front wheel of Jackson's bike buckled as it rammed the side of the van. Jackson catapulted over his handlebars and slammed head first into the sliding door on the side of the vehicle.

He was unconscious before he hit the road.

Jackson saw the yellow strip lights first, passing like a night train.

He could hear the squeak of the tiny wheels under the trolley he believed he was lying on, and felt the cold chrome of its framework under his forearm. The faceless silhouettes of the people pushing him blocked the lights for a moment and then vanished. He heard voices, but they had no meaning and he was too dizzy to concentrate on them.

Suddenly the lights were much brighter – almost white – illuminating the whole space. Faces, obscured behind masks, peered over him. The prick of a needle caused a searing pain in his forehead, but then he was sure it was followed by someone saying his name. The voice was familiar, but in his hazy stupor Jackson couldn't make the connection. The face of a surgeon, with a clinical mask on, slowly came into focus.

'You had a nasty cut on your head, Jackson.'

That's reassuring, thought Jackson. *He knows my name.*

'I'm going to stitch it up, best I can,' the man continued.

'*Best I can?*' Jackson contemplated. *Less reassuring.* And that voice – a memory from the past that, try as he might, Jackson was just too groggy to place.

The surgeon removed the cotton mask around his mouth and smiled.

'You've been asleep for a while – but you need to sleep more. You should start to feel the effects of the anaesthetic I've given you kick in.'

Anaesthetic? Jackson forced his delirious head around

the word. Good, at least he wouldn't have to endure the pain in his forehead for much longer – damn, it hurt.

It was hard to see the surgeon clearly, the light above him was so bright, but what a face he had. Either the drugs were affecting his eyes, or this was one seriously ugly doctor. The harsh lights cast shadows in the deep furrows of skin on the man's cheeks and nose. If Jackson had to describe his surgeon's appearance, he would say that his face looked like it had melted.

Then the man was gone and Jackson's eyelids felt too heavy to keep from closing.

Jackson's sleep was fitful. Several times he thought he was awake, watching the surgeon attending to his fore-head, feeling the sharp pain of a needle, but then the room would merge with memories of people and places until everything blacked out.

Jackson knew when he was properly awake. The lights weren't so harsh, he could feel the aches in his body and the way the skin on his forehead tugged and felt tight around what he suspected were stitches.

'You're awake!'

The voice of the surgeon was startling. Jackson didn't even know he was sitting next to his bed.

Jackson turned to see him, but nothing could have prepared him for what he saw.

Rising from the chair with a smile was the man who

had tended to Jackson for however long he'd been in this place. But this man was no surgeon. Now that Jackson was completely clearheaded, even the melted skin on the face of the man couldn't distract him from his conclusion. That voice. Those eyes. It was Devlin Lear!

Jackson instinctively tried to get up. But a strap across his stomach kept him secured to the bed, and both his arms were also tied down with rope.

'I apologize for the need to strap you down, Jackson,' Lear said. 'I figured you might find my presence a little ... alarming.'

Even though Jackson himself had concluded that Lear was still alive, he was astonished to be looking at him. 'What the hell are you doing?' he said, pain pulsing from the wound on his forehead.

'I could ask you the same question,' Lear replied. 'Or, rather, what were you about to do? Do you think I could have let you pass on what you know?'

'I don't know what you're talking about.'

'Please, let's not play games,' Lear continued. 'I've been watching you, Jackson. *Manual of Mineralogy*? I thought Miss English was the only one who was into rock! And I've been looking over your shoulder while you surfed all those pathetic sightings of me.'

Jackson shivered. How could he know? Brooke had designed her handsets with high-level encryption. There was virtually no way anyone could be sniffing the data on them. Jackson's heart sank as he realized – anyone but Lear.

'You've been focusing on my swarm!' said Lear, in that uncanny way Jackson remembered he had of almost mind reading. 'But a single small silent robot can be extremely useful when snooping.' Lear mouthed each word slowly in a sibilant whisper – Jackson also remembered his liking for theatrics and the sound of his own voice. Jackson was too amazed to say anything.

'In your dorm building, in the Englishs' laboratory – just one of my machines enables me to see what you're seeing on those clever phones of yours and listen to your conversations.'

'So what next?' Jackson stuttered. 'You going to kill me?'

Lear let out a spontaneous laugh. 'I'd certainly be justified, wouldn't you say, Farley?' Then his countenance changed, becoming darker. 'When you and English betrayed my trust, things became extremely difficult for me. The empire I'd sweated blood to build had crumbled. Even after my disappearing act, the scavengers continued to pick the meat from my bones. Corporations that had stood side by side with me, and governments who had contracted MeX to do their dirty work, all stood in line for whatever morsels they could strip from the skeleton of Lear Corp.'

Lear walked to a table across from Jackson's bed and

picked up something from a silver tray. As he held it, the blade of a scalpel flashed in the light.

Jackson's whole body went rigid.

'As you suspected, Farley, I decided to make use of the *openness* of certain South American countries to visitors who want to keep a low profile. Even so, I couldn't stop sightings of me appearing on the Internet. So I decided to go under the surgeon's knife.'

Lear drew the scalpel blade across his face, just millimetres from his skin.

'But the imbecile who tried to change me got it wrong!' Lear's eyes burned with rage and he stabbed the scalpel down, its blade snapping on the surface of the metal table. 'The infection he gave me ate my face. If I hadn't had the vile tissue cut away, it would have killed me.'

Jackson could see beads of sweat forming on Lear's forehead, but not on the undulating ridges of shiny skin that bubbled up around his cheeks and nose – those remained shiny and plastic-looking.

'What can I say?' Lear's mood seemed to lighten. 'I wouldn't recommend visiting this particular plastic surgeon – not that he has a hospital left to visit.'

Jackson dared not think what Lear meant by that last comment.

'So now we come to the diamonds, Farley. For thousands of years, so many stones, so much blood. It's hard to put your finger on what it is about gemstones that so enchants. Coloured ones are especially beguiling. As your scrawny little geologist friend would attest, the most valuable diamonds in the world are naturally occurring coloured ones. But as we both know, Farley, science is amazing and if you can convince a buyer that your isotope-bombarded rocks are naturally coloured – well, he'll go to the ends of the earth to get his hands on them.'

'So the diamonds your swarm stole from Brazil are sitting in MIT's reactor right now?'

'What a clever boy you are. It's a shame you've always been so . . . idealistic, shall we say.'

Lear walked up to the metal table, where a tube that snaked into Jackson's arm terminated in a bag of fluid. Lear turned a small tap underneath the bag, then smiled back at Jackson.

'I think you should stay here for a little while,' he said. 'For your own safety, Farley, you understand. When you wake up, both I and my new blue diamonds will be gone – and, as the dust settles, the last thing the authorities will be concerned about is some English kid chasing a ghost.'

Jackson could feel the effects of whatever was flowing into his veins from the tube in his arm. The lights seemed brighter again and his head felt light.

Lear stood at Jackson's bedside for a moment, just watching him. 'Goodbye, Jackson,' he whispered, then he turned and walked out.

All Jackson's body craved was to give in to the effects of the inebriating liquid that was mixing with his blood, and to drift into a deep sleep. But he fought it – he had to if he was going to get out of here alive.

Shifting his weight from side to side, he started to rock the bed sideways towards the metal table. Something gave on the wheels underneath, a brake perhaps, because now the bed moved more easily. Quickly, Jackson bent his right arm at the elbow and reached out his hand to yank the tube from the bag that fed it. As the clear liquid drug drained from the bag and on to the table, he saw it was pooling around his phone, which had obviously been removed from his pocket and switched off. Next to it sat the broken scalpel.

Jackson stretched and grabbed the scalpel between the tips of his fingers. Most of the instrument's metal blade was missing, but a chunk at the base was left.

The room was spinning now and he felt as if he was holding on to the side of a carousel. He sliced the stub of the scalpel blade across the rope holding down his arm and somehow managed to drunkenly sever the rope without lacerating himself in the process.

With his free hand, he clumsily unclipped the belt round his waist and slipped his other arm free. As he dropped to the floor, his legs almost gave way, but Jackson wouldn't let them – he grabbed his phone and drew a circle with it in the air, the gesture that switched it back on.

Giddy from not only the drugs but also relief at escaping the horrendous room, Jackson stumbled through the surgery doors into the corridor. His jelly legs carried him as quickly as they could, past doors in other rooms, towards what he hoped was the exit, when he heard someone shout from behind him. He knew that voice and this time it wasn't Lear.

Jackson looked round in horror and his fears were confirmed. It was Goulman – and he didn't look as if he was there to help him.

Jackson rattled the handle of the door nearest to him, but it was locked. He ran to the next one as Goulman ate up the corridor with his large strides, and almost cried with relief as this one opened and Jackson fell in, locking it instantly.

There was a roar of anger from outside. 'Lear! Get someone to find the key for this room! He's locked himself inside.'

Jackson couldn't believe it – what on earth were Goulman and Lear doing working together? This nightmare was getting worse by the minute.

As key after key was tried, Jackson knew it was a matter of seconds before his captors entered his temporary refuge. He could try to call Brooke, but if she wasn't by her phone it might take her a while to answer. Besides, his phone would be checked and then he'd just be moved on to another location. Jackson made a lightning-quick calculation in his head as his fingers stroked the device's glossy plastic surface and stabbed at the SMS application.

He focused all his energy into his fingers as they quickly punched number and letter combinations into his phone.

**C5 C4 D5 D3 F5 F4 F3 G4 H4 H3 J4 K5 K3 L4
N5 N4 O3 P5 P4 R5 R4 R3 S3**

With the entry finished, Jackson hit SEND. As he began to lose consciousness, the last he heard was the crash of the door flying open and the voices of Goulman and Lear.

'Check where it was sent!'

'It just clicks! It's a dead line. It must be the drugs; he's just typed a load of gibberish.'

'Good. Put him back in the storeroom. And make sure you lock it this time!'

CHAPTER 18

It had been twenty-four hours since Brooke had last had contact with Jackson.

It was very strange. Even when Jackson needed some space after his dad's visit, he'd texted to say he was OK. Something was very wrong.

Brooke had had no luck with his phone, finding it switched off every time she called. So she'd got the number for Atticus79 from the janitor of their building and had arranged to go round and see him.

If Atticus79 didn't come up with anything useful, Brooke thought, as she rounded the corner to Simmons Hall, she would go to the police. The irony of asking the very people who had wrongly accused her father of terrorism didn't escape her, but it might just be her only option.

When Brooke reached the building, she noticed a small crowd of students gathered outside, pointing up at the front of the building.

Brooke looked herself and saw what was causing all

the fuss. Unusually, considering it was dark, most of the building's lights were out, except for a few glowing in windows in the centre of the huge structure, which seemed to form a pattern.

'Ghoul!' said Atticus79.

Brooke hadn't even noticed him.

'It doesn't make sense!' the gaunt boy continued. 'There's no point doing a hack if no one understands what you're trying to say.'

Now Atticus79 mentioned it, the lit windows did form crude letters, which spelled *Ghoul*.

Brooke stared open-mouthed at the towering matrix of lights. She was in no doubt that the message had come from Jackson.

As Brooke entered the lab, she made straight for Goulman's desk. She felt guilty about snooping in her dad's lab assistant's things, but Ghoul wasn't here for her to ask questions about Jackson and it was unlikely that he'd be back before the morning.

Atticus79's account of Jackson asking about diamonds had given Brooke no further clues to what Jackson meant by his message, and so Ghoul – or in this case his laptop – was her only chance of finding any information about her missing friend.

But just as she booted up his machine, Brooke heard the sound of footsteps in the stairwell. She could tell from the energetic way the feet pounded the stairs that it was Goulman.

'Shucks!' she said under her breath, promptly shutting the laptop and checking that nothing else was out of place on his desk. She wasn't sure she needed to be hiding anything but she felt guilty for poking about nonetheless.

'Hi, Brooke!' said Goulman nonchalantly as he entered the lab. 'How's J.P. doing? That lawyer of his made any progress?'

'He's good,' said Brooke, moving away from Goulman's desk. 'The lawyer says the police investigation has fallen apart. Dad should be released tomorrow!' Goulman walked to his desk. He opened a drawer and transferred a few things from it to a holdall. Brooke squinted, but couldn't see what things exactly he was loading into the bag. Goulman felt Brooke's eyes on him and turned.

'Um, I'm outta here, Brooke,' he said. 'I might work from home for a few days.' Then he corrected himself. 'Unless of course there's anything you need me to do for J.P.?'

'Er, no,' Brooke said. 'Working from home should be fine.'

The last thing Goulman packed was his laptop. 'See ya later!' he said, scooping up the bag full of stuff with one large powerful arm and striding towards the stairs. And then he was gone.

That was strange, thought Brooke. Goulman hadn't

seemed as pleased as she had expected at the news that J.P. was about to be released – in fact, he hadn't commented on it at all. And he'd been so keen to get in and out of the lab quickly, she hadn't even had a chance to ask him about Jackson.

Brooke felt a mixture of confusion and guilt. She didn't want to be feeling suspicious of a man she'd known and trusted for years, but something just wasn't right here. And Jackson was still missing.

Brooke turned to the robot pens.

Tread hardly made a whisper as he cruised fifteen metres behind Goulman's station wagon.

One of the advantages of the wheel-bot's two-stage, hybrid fuel-cell engine, which J.P. had made sure to explain to the government funding agencies, was that it was whisper quiet. Stealth was something the professor had always felt was missing from high-speed police pursuit vehicles. If a car-jacker didn't know anyone was following him, so J.P.'s pitch went, there was no need for the criminal to speed. That made him safer to the public and easier to catch.

Brooke followed *Tread* in *Tin Lizzie* – *Tug* and *Fist* were stowed inside the trunk. She kept her distance, as she didn't want to risk Goulman spotting her in his rear-view mirror. It was around 11 p.m. and there weren't too many other cars on the road, but via *Tread*'s camera Brooke had noticed one or two pedestrians and a guy on a bicycle double take as *Tread* glided noiselessly past them.

Crucially, Goulman hadn't clocked a thing as he wormed his way through Cambridge and, so far, he looked as if he was just going home. That is, until he turned left when he should have taken a right. Instead of picking up the expressway out of the city, he was travelling to the other side of the university campus.

The station wagon descended down a service road and pulled up at the bottom, beside steel double doors. Brooke knew immediately where on the campus they were – the ramp led down to the storage facilities and access tunnels beneath one of the huge chemistry blocks. When the gas tanks and chemical feeds that supplied the laboratories in the building needed servicing, this was where the maintenance staff drove in.

Brooke watched *Tread*'s feed on the screen that was built into *Tin Lizzie*'s dashboard. The door opened and a man stepped out. He turned, threaded a chain through the handles of the doors and padlocked its two ends together.

As the man climbed into Goulman's car, Brooke strained to see if she recognized him, but the brim of his hat cast a harsh shadow over his face.

The station wagon then drove forwards and up the ramp, bearing left at the top and joining the main road.

Brooke intended to let *Tread* follow the men, but as

she drifted down the ramp and past the steel doors, she saw that they were fire doors – doors designed to open out in the event of a laboratory blaze.

Why would you lock a fire door? she thought. *To keep someone from getting out!*

As Brooke manipulated the thin white plastic handset in her hand, *Fist* jumped from *Tin Lizzie*'s trunk. Seconds later the chain and padlock lay in tatters. *Fist* made short work of the fireproof doors too, bending back the toughened steel.

Without a single window in the concrete maze of tunnels, it was pitch black, but *Tread*'s powerful LED beam lit up the subterranean tunnels as Brooke scurried after her uni-wheeled machine, *Fist* walking faithfully behind on his fingertips.

Fist must have smashed down the doors of twenty different rooms before Brooke heard the faint trace of a voice in the dark.

'Jackson!' Brooke burst into one of the rooms, horrified to find her friend delirious and handcuffed to a bed.

As *Fist* carried him to her waiting Hummer, Jackson was muttering jumbled words.

'Dust!' he mumbled. 'Diamond . . . dust!'

'I don't know what's going on, Jackson,' said Brooke, jumping into the driving seat. 'But you're going to the hospital! Look at the state of your head! It looks like you were sewn up by a three-year-old.'

'No!' he groaned. 'Not hospital. No time!'

'Why's there no time, Jackson?' Brooke asked. She looked round; there didn't seem to be anyone coming after them. What was it Jackson was trying to tell her?

'Dust . . .' he tried again. 'He's going to do it, when the . . . the dust settles.'

'What dust? Who?' asked Brooke gently.

'Dust . . . the radioactive dust. Dust from the bomb.' Jackson took a deep breath, desperately trying one last time to speak sense through the effects of the drugs. 'Lear's put a bomb in the reactor.'

Tin Lizzie skidded sideways through the crossroads as Brooke gripped the steering wheel with white knuckles. Jackson's drugs were slowly wearing off and he had managed to explain, with some difficulty, about Goulman's betrayal and, even worse, Lear's reappearance in their life.

'He done fooled us all!' said Brooke. 'That evil scumbag just doesn't know when to lie down and accept defeat.' She really had believed he'd been dead all this time.

They were too late to prevent Lear's diamond theft from the reactor, but their main concern now was to stop the explosion that Lear and Goulman had set up to cover their tracks and distract the authorities from pursuing them.

Brooke accelerated up the street where MIT's nuclear reactor was. As the self-driving Hummer passed the building, with her tachometer touching 70 kilometres an hour, Brooke kicked open the tailgate and *Tug* and *Fist* dropped out.

Tin Lizzie continued on to the basement of the Fire Proof building as Brooke, still in the driving seat, targeted the reactor complex's front door through *Tug*'s camera.

'FLTTN IT' read her text command.

'MY PLESUR ;-)' came *Tug*'s reply.

No sooner had Brooke's handset warmed to *Tug*'s response, than the snubnosed robot had shot across the road and demolished the armour-plated door.

'SRCH AN DSCVR,' texted Brooke, sending the robot on an automated tour of the reactor plant. Then *Tin Lizzie* arrived outside the entrance to the lift in the Fire Proof building. Jackson was feeling much better, but he was in no state to control a robot. As they descended in the lift cage down to the lab, Brooke helped him from her Hummer. Once in the basement, she sat him in a workstation chair, then ran to her own desk.

Transferring *Tug*'s video feed to the widescreen monitor on her desk, Brooke could see two guards in a corridor, holding their stomachs in agony.

'It's the Bass Bombs,' said Jackson. 'Lear's swarm robots are fitted with Bass Bombs.'

'We'll come back for them later,' said Brooke. 'We need to check the main building first.'

With *Tug* leading the way on autopilot, Brooke directed *Fist* to follow him.

The rhythmic blinking of yellow warning lights revealed a curved corridor, which ran, moat-like, round the concrete dome inside which the reactor core was housed.

'It's eerie,' whispered Jackson. His head was throbbing, but he was feeling more alert.

'It's also deadly,' said Brooke. 'Look at that reading.' Brooke pointed at her 32-inch LED monitor, which was showing what looked like a rectangular clock on the concrete wall of the reactor corridor. 'It's a Geiger counter. It measures ionizing radiation. And it's showing lethal levels. Anyone in this building is in terrible danger.'

'What about the guards?' Jackson rasped. 'There is nothing between them and the reactor.'

'*Fist* can get the guards out,' said Brooke. '*Tug* is best set up to check on the reactor core. Do you think you can manage him?'

'I can try,' said Jackson.

Tug was still in his automated discovery mode as he entered the circular corridor that ringed the reactor. He was halfway round the concrete-lined passage when his camera locked on to some rubble, below a hole cut out of the inside wall. Jackson could clearly see that the uneven edge of the hole was made up of other, much smaller circles.

'The hole in the reactor wall has been reopened!' Jackson croaked. 'I'm switching *Tug* to manual.'

As *Tug* passed through the hole in the thick concrete and entered the nuclear chamber, his video feed became hazy. Jackson, whose own vision was still a little blurry, squinted as waves of static flowed across his display. *Tug* himself began to become unstable; his engines surged in fitful bursts and his gyros twitched as if his presence in the toxic chamber was making him nervous.

Suddenly, through the ripples of white noise on his display, Jackson saw two blue plastic barrels, held together by straps, with some sort of electronic device secured to the top of them. He moved *Tug* slowly forward, until he could make out a small black electronic device. He had to wait for the foggy video feed to clear several times before he understood what he was looking at. Sitting on top of a larger plastic box, which in turn was wired into the plastic barrels, was an iPod with six figures on its colour screen, counting down: 00.00.48.

'We've got less than a minute before this whole building goes up and all that radiation is released into the air!' shouted Jackson.

'All right already, I'm on it!' Brooke snapped, as she tried to focus fully on the job of hooking two of *Fist*'s fingerlike grapplers round the belts of the two security guards.

With the guards hitched securely, *Fist* started dragging the men back down the passageway.

Jackson stared at the improvised bomb. It reminded him of a situation he'd been in once before, in a Cambodian village with MeX. They couldn't even see the bombs that needed defusing back then, but actually, this situation, with *Tug* hovering only ten centimetres from one, was no easier. He couldn't risk the tactic they'd used in Cambodia, a controlled explosion, because the blast would throw thousands of pieces of radioactive debris on to the streets around the reactor.

His only hope was to try and move the bomb to reduce its impact on the core.

Jackson gently raised the wrist of his phone hand and *Tug* instantly responded, floating up and over the bomb, dropping in between it and the core itself – a tall concrete column, clad in aluminium strips, which stood in the middle of the chamber. Jackson waited for a pulse of pain from the slash on his head to weaken, then he edged *Tug* forward until the nose of the robot was touching the middle of the two blue drums.

Hardly daring to breathe, Jackson gestured for *Tug* to push.

To his relief, the bomb began to slide easily towards the hole in the reactor chamber, but almost as soon as the drums jerked forward Jackson thought he heard a voice.

'Tut, tut. Where is your appreciation of drama, Mr Farley?' To Jackson's amazement it was the unmistakable voice of Devlin Lear. He obviously wasn't there, so where was the pre-recording coming from?

Jackson rolled *Tug* back up and over the bomb in order

to get a view of the iPod's screen and looked in disbelief at the face he'd hoped never to see again – Lear.

Displayed on the iPod's small screen, Lear continued. 'I hope you appreciate the dramatic irony of you being the cause of the explosion you're trying to stop. As soon as you moved my device, the inertial trigger in this clever little music player sensed the vibration and cued this pre-recorded monologue. And now, like all great perform- ances, this one must end with a bang!'

Jackson scarcely had time to register what Lear was saying before there was an almighty boom!

The enormous explosion in the reactor shook the foundations of even J.P.'s blast-shielded lab, tiny frag- ments of dust and plaster floating down around Brooke and Jackson from the laboratory ceiling.

'Tell me you got those guards out of there!' said Jack- son.

'They're underneath the parking ramp across the street,' said Brooke. 'They're conscious, but they could definitely do with a doc!'

'I have a feeling they'll be getting one very soon – along with every emergency vehicle in Massachusetts.'

'And *Tug*?' asked Brooke.

'He's gone,' said Jackson.

CHAPTER 20

Even before the radioactive dust from the blast had settled, Brooke and Jackson had loaded everything they could lay their hands on from the lab into *Tin Lizzie*: *Tread*, *Verne*, *Fist*, the automated Chauffeur, flight cases full of tools and materials, transceivers, batteries and chargers, and some papers from Goulman's desk. They had no choice; the streets around the reactor had been rendered deadly by the irradiated debris strewn all over them. And not even the lab was safe from the radioactive particles that would be blowing around for some time to come.

Brooke was fuming, and when everything had gone into the Hummer's boot – except for *Tug* – Jackson had seen her eyes well up with tears. To Brooke, all her robots were like family members. She had sped out of the Fire Proof building, past the disaster scene of burning rubble, and had carried on at the same breakneck speed for at least twenty minutes north out of Cambridge before Jackson managed to persuade her to ease off the throttle and stop running red lights.

'We're safe now, Brooke,' Jackson said softly. 'The radioactivity will be localized to a few blocks around the reactor.' But he knew this wasn't the real reason she'd been driving like a maniac. 'I'm really sorry about *Tug*,' he added.

'We need to know what's going on!' Brooke snapped.

She pushed a button on the dashboard and a small TV monitor popped up. Then she poked the touchscreen and moved up through the channels until she reached one showing a reporter sitting in a helicopter.

'We are coming to you live from the skies over Cambridge,' shouted the chisel-jawed man over the noise of the helicopter. 'MIT's reactor is burning! Police are evacuating an area the length of Massachusetts Avenue and asking anyone within five blocks of the reactor to leave the area. Hazardous Material specialists, drafted in for the previous attack on the reactor, are already combing the wreckage. In the last five minutes, the police commissioner made this statement.'

The picture changed to a shot of an important-looking officer in uniform, surrounded by a crush of reporters with microphones and cameras.

'It is too early to confirm whether this explosion is related to the earlier incident at the university's reactor,' he said, looking at the throng of reporters. 'But we are investigating links to a suspect, currently being held in custody, MIT professor, J.P. English.'

'My God,' Brooke stammered. 'This doesn't get any better, does it?'

Jackson too couldn't imagine a more disastrous turn of events.

A pushy reporter shouted a question at the officer. 'How could Professor English have pulled this off while in police custody?'

'We believe he had help,' the officer replied. 'We have issued a warrant for the arrest of Mr English's daughter, Brooke English, and British MIT student Jackson Farley, thought to be studying under the professor.'

Jackson and Brooke sat in stunned silence.

The newscast flicked back to the reporter inside the helicopter. 'BBN News can exclusively reveal this CCTV footage of a vehicle racing away from the scene of the explosion.'

Brooke and Jackson watched, aghast, as a clearly recognizable *Tin Lizzie* skidded round the corner of the Metropolitan Storage building and shot up the road.

'Well, that's just peachy!' said Brooke, turning into an alleyway behind a large tenement block and guiding the Hummer around a succession of rubbish carts. 'If the Feds lock us up, who's gonna prove my dad's innocence?'

'Lear!' said Jackson, through gritted teeth. 'He's planning to sell the diamonds somewhere. If we can find out where, we can end all of this.'

'Given the circumstances, you and I being fugitives and

all, and my dad's hope of release looking decidedly dodgy, don't you think we should leave Lear to his own devices?'

'He's the only one who has all the answers to this whole mess,' insisted Jackson.

'Well, the guy's managed to come back from the dead and turn us and my father into America's Most Wanted. When a guy like that wants to vanish, chances are he'll stay vanished.'

'Not necessarily,' said Jackson, staring blankly at the road ahead. 'I've got an idea.'

The apartment was a shambles.

'This is perfect – just what I was thinking about,' Jackson said, satisfied. Every possible opportunity for storage had been used. Every shelf and every surface in the room was covered in towering piles of books and journals. 'And this Mr Zeal lets you use this apartment whenever you want?'

'Sure, him and my dad are old buddies from their college days. He leaves a key under the front doormat. He's hardly ever in town and when he's not around he lets me use it, when J.P. and I have had a fall out.'

Brooke fell quiet as she thought about her dad.

'Well, it's the perfect hideout for two renegades on the run from the law,' Jackson declared in an action-hero voice. He checked to see if he'd made Brooke smile at all. 'And it's got all the kit we need to take over the world. Just check out the retro computer!'

The antique-looking Apple Mac sat on a desk, in very close proximity to several large boxes. One of the boxes contained fossils and the other two potted plants.

'He should box up that old thing with these other relics,' said Brooke as she removed some kind of fossil from one of the boxes and waved it at Jackson.

'What are you talking about?' Jackson laughed. 'My school still uses this model!' Sadly, he was being serious.

'Lucky for you, then, that I got you out of there,' said Brooke.

Jackson didn't feel lucky. On the run from the FBI. His arch-nemesis Lear back from the dead. No father. *Actually, I take that back*, he thought, feeling guilty. Mr Farley had sent a frantic text to Jackson, trying to find out where he was and if he was OK, as soon as the details of the MIT explosion hit the news. He had only just managed to persuade his dad not to come across and find his fugitive-on-the-run son, assuring him that he was fine, with Brooke, and would explain all very soon. Luckily, he still had some favours owed after everything that had happened between the two of them.

'So, what's your big idea?' asked Brooke as they sat down in front of the computer.

'Bayesian analysis!' said Jackson.

'It's never a good sign when I'm lost before you even begin,' said Brooke.

'The Markov chain? The random walk? Probability theory?' said Jackson.

'Still not registering!' said Brooke, completely bemused.

'They are branches of mathematics which allow us to analyse past events so that, in theory at least, we might predict future ones. We all like to think we are in control of our own fate, that we decide the direction in which we go, how far we travel, how long we take to get there. But there are patterns in our behaviour that can some-times be quantified into equations.'

'I'm getting that brain-ache thing I told you about. Would you get to the point, please?'

'Take you and me. We didn't choose to be in this apart-ment tonight; a pattern of events has brought us here. By evaluating the pieces of that pattern, we can guess at where we might be going to next.'

'Well, I'm going to cross this room and bury you under a pile of these dusty ol' books if you don't start speaking in proper sentences soon.'

Jackson sighed. 'Just stick with me for one more minute.'

Brooke looked sceptical but said nothing.

'How tall is the guy who owns this apartment?' asked Jackson.

'Mr Zeal? I guess he's about your height,' said Brooke as she cleared a cluster of popcorn boxes and encrusted plastic TV dinner trays from the sofa.

'That makes things nice and easy,' said Jackson. 'OK, see that scarf?' He pointed at a black-and-white checked woollen scarf which had been dropped in the middle of the floor. 'If I draw a circle round it, I can begin to build up a picture of where its owner was standing when he dropped it.'

Jackson crouched down over the black-and-white scarf and extended his right arm. He then spun round, allowing the chalk in his hand to draw a large circle on the dark wooden floor.

'Look,' said Jackson. 'The circle passes too close to the bookshelf for its owner to have stood there – that's one variable. The same is true of its proximity to the couch, the desk and the breakfast bar. So, he must have been standing here.'

Jackson stepped backwards into the corridor between the sitting room and the kitchen.

'If I draw circles round every discarded object in this room and then subtract the points where it's impossible to stand, I have a good chance of predicting the behaviour of your dad's friend, next time he comes home.'

'I can predict that too,' added Brooke. 'He's going to be freaked out that someone has drawn chalk circles round all his stuff!'

'Just as well then, that maths means I don't need to draw actual circles. I can create an algorithm, which will draw them for me!'

'Jackson, how is all this going to help my dad?'

'With probability theory, it's possible we can work out where Lear is heading next!'

For the first time since they'd arrived in the apartment, Brooke began listening.

'First, I need the variables. I need you to tell me every piece of information we have about Lear's journey to Boston. Where we know he visited, where we think he might have visited and anywhere along the route that may be of relevance to him, like the location of diamond mines.'

'Something tells me I ain't gonna get time to see my appearance on the news again,' said Brooke, despondently waving the TV remote control.

Brooke entered 'Lear +sighting' into the search engine and punched the ENTER key on Mr Zeal's grubby keyboard, trying not to touch it any more than was necessary. The Apple Mac's ancient hard drive purred and after a few seconds the screen revealed the first twelve of 68,600 possible results.

Brooke quickly found a reference to Lear and the capital city of Paraguay. She read out the text below a large photograph of a man in a panama hat, shot from behind him.

'It's from the *Paraguay Post*', she called over to Jackson. 'According to a source within the national police headquarters in Asunción, Paraguay, there have been reported sightings of a man fitting the description of missing Inter-net billionaire Devlin Lear. Lear is wanted by the international criminal police organization INTERPOL in connection with a number of anonymously posted Internet videos.'

Brooke glanced knowingly at Jackson, who winked and smiled back – in a very un-anonymous way.

She read on. '*If the videos are proven to be authentic, Lear could face life in prison for his part in an illegal cartel which allegedly used violence and bribery to trade stolen water in Eastern Europe.* He was reported lost at sea, three weeks after that article was published,' Brooke concluded. 'In fact, here's something about it.'

On the screen was another article from the *Paraguay Post* website. It was one that Jackson remembered. It had been his first glimmer of hope that Lear wouldn't be coming after him any more.

'Any indication of where his yacht was when they think it sank?'

'It says that coastguards searched an area off the east-ern coast of Brazil,' said Brooke.

'You can see,' said Jackson, pointing to a picture that accompanied the Internet news article. 'If he made it to Brazil, there are a number of ways he could have gone on to Paraguay. So I think it's safe to say that the sighting of him in Paraguay is a good place to start.'

Jackson walked to the kitchen and wrote 'Asunción,

Paraguay' on the fridge blackboard. Doing something productive began to calm him down.

'The article quotes witnesses who say they saw Lear's boat being repaired in a boatyard near Buenos Aires before it went missing.'

Jackson chalked up 'Buenos Aires, Argentina' on the board. 'Now we need to add the numbers,' he said. 'Has he got Google Earth on that thing?'

'Yessir,' said Brooke, opening the program.

'Good. It's got a virtual ruler. You can use it to measure the distance between places.'

The decrepit Mac groaned for the best part of a minute as the program slowly materialized, and Brooke entered 'Asunción, Paraguay' into the FLY TO box. They both watched as the virtual globe revolved and Paraguay filled the screen.

'Now imagine you're in Lear's yacht; use the ruler tool to drag a route down the Paraguay river until you find your way out to the Atlantic Ocean,' Jackson instructed. 'What have we got?'

Brooke read out the results. 'The distance from Paraguay's capital city, to Buenos Aires, at the mouth of the Atlantic where his yacht was seen, is 1,600 kilometres.'

Jackson wrote '1,600 km' next to 'Buenos Aires' on the blackboard.

'One down!' said Brooke triumphantly. 'Now where next?'

Jackson was staring at the glistening Atlantic coastline that covered the entire surface of Brooke's screen, his finger tracing the names of ports.

'Wait a minute!' he said as his finger hovered over Rio de Janeiro. 'What about Goulman? We know he was working with Lear and we know he visited Rio a few weeks ago because he brought you back a carnival T-shirt!'

'So Goulman wasn't on holiday at all – he picked up Lear and his robots on his yacht and brought him to Boston!'

'Yes, and I'm guessing they stopped off at a port near the Brazilian diamond mine to let Lear's robots help themselves to the shipment of white diamonds.'

The pair continued to work through everything they could find relating to glimpses of Lear since his supposed death. Brooke also introduced some credit-card statements she'd managed to lift from Goulman's desk, which confirmed two locations he'd docked and taken on fuel in Venezuela and Florida.

After an hour of searching and cross-checking, Jackson had written a list of confirmed sightings and stop-offs on the blackboard.

- Asunción, Paraguay, to Buenos Aires (1,600 km)
- Buenos Aires to Rio de Janeiro (1,980 km)
- Rio de Janeiro to Sao Luis, Brazil (3,494 km)
- Sao Luis, Brazil, to Maracaibo, Venezuela (3,667 km)

- Maracaibo, Venezuela, to Sanibel Island, Florida (3,036 km)
- Sanibel Island, Florida, to Wilmington, North Carolina (1,504 km)
- Wilmington, North Carolina, to Boston, Massachusetts (1,490 km)

'Good! Now my algorithm should give us the probability of Lear's next jump,' said Jackson.

He dropped into a squat and started to feverishly chalk a series of figures and algorithmic arrows and boxes on the black wooden floor. A matrix of flashing markers formed in his head, a series of shimmering beacons, shining out from a sea of numbers and a coastline made of lines and angles. Next to each location he saw a single-digit number, a value, which denoted its importance: 6 for Paraguay where Lear had blown up the hospital, 7s and 8s for Rio de Janeiro and the diamond mine that branched out around it, and 9, the highest score possible, for the city of Boston where Lear had left MIT's reactor in bits. Before long, the floor was covered in Jackson's jottings.

'That should do it,' said Jackson, standing up and stretching his back muscles. 'Draw a line from Boston that's this long.' Jackson pointed with his toe at a four-figure number scrawled on the floor in chalk. '2,017 kilometres in length, anywhere along an arc from north-east to north-west.'

'Why do you think Lear is going north? Might he just turn round and go back where he came from?'

'Not according to probability,' Jackson replied confidently.

Brooke used the Google Earth program to draw a line the length and direction Jackson had specified. 'It doesn't touch anything,' she said. 'Except water.'

'What do you mean?' said Jackson, surprised. 'It should show a port. Somewhere on that arc there should be a port where Lear and Goulman are headed.'

Jackson looked at the monitor and, sure enough, the line terminated in the Atlantic Ocean.

'If you ask me,' Brooke said as she walked to the kitchen, 'there's a strong probability that your probability theory is wrong.'

'Something's not right here,' mumbled Jackson, his attention caught between the computer screen and the scribbles on the floor.

'Yep, your numbers aren't right,' replied Brooke, with her head inside a kitchen cupboard. 'It's not all bad news, though. At least we've got some potato chips!'

'No!' snapped Jackson. His frustration was getting the better of him. 'The problem is with the data you gave me! It's obvious that all of the sightings fit within a pattern. Except these two.'

Jackson was back in front of the fridge, pointing at the numbers next to Buenos Aires, Argentina, and Wilmington, North Carolina. 'These numbers don't fit within the pattern; there isn't enough distance between them. Bring their details up again,' demanded Jackson.

'Did anyone ever tell you that you're a tyrant!' said Brooke, through a mouthful of crisps. She sat back at the desk and clicked the HISTORY tab on her browser, selecting the relevant pages.

'Read them again – all of them,' insisted Jackson. 'This time, tell me if there's anything in there that stands out.'

Brooke scowled at Jackson and then flicked back to the article about the Buenos Aires sighting.

'I guess *this* is a bit suspicious.' She frowned, reading from the screen. 'In a separate report, Señora Ramírez, 73, was questioned by Buenos Aires provincial police, when she claimed she had seen Elvis working in the gas station at the Puerto Madero Holiday Community. Police Detective Alandra Lopez said she had investigated the señora's claim that the dead star was alive and well, only because the elderly lady was so convincing. During a thorough inspection of the gas station and holiday trailer park, no man fitting the king of rock and roll's description was found.

'The old doll's a fruitcake!' said Brooke.

'Now check the other story,' demanded Jackson.

Brooke switched to the blog of 'Cathy Cool' and looked over the post entitled 'Lear's living in Wilmington!' She then scanned further down the page, looking briefly through the blog posts below it. Finally, she chose one to read out. The short story contained a picture of a piece of toast with the headline 'Holy Toast' written above it.

The accompanying text told how the blogger had taken out a slice of bread from her toaster that morning and, to her amazement, discovered 'a perfect depiction of the face of my recently deceased dog, Mr Tippins, burned into the surface of the bread'. She went on to say that, over the last few years, she had seen other spirits in her toast and the bodies of aliens formed in potatoes and other vegetables.

'I see dead people,' said Brooke, her eyes as wide as a zombie's.

'Yeah, and I think I see the problem with my algorithm – it contains two false sightings!' replied Jackson.

With the knowledge that Lear had never stopped at Buenos Aires or Wilmington, Brooke took new measurements, which Jackson quickly absorbed into his ever-expanding floor sum. Finally, he wrote '4,147 km' on the black wooden floorboards, where '2,017 km' had been.

'Now, within that arc, there's a bunch of places he could make for,' said Brooke. 'Crossing the Atlantic wouldn't fit within the pattern; it's about a thousand kilometres too far away. There's Greenland, but there ain't nothing there for him – just a bunch of icebergs and polar bears. But if we bend the line west, into the Hudson Bay, the coast of Canada is the perfect distance away.'

'Canada?' Something sparked in Jackson's memory. It was the book Atticus79 had shown him, featuring the locations of the world's diamond mines. 'That's it! The probability fits – he's heading to a diamond mine in Canada!'

'Are you sure?' Brooke didn't sound convinced. 'Let me see how many diamond mines there are in Canada.' She did a search for 'Canadian diamond mines' and seconds later the two of them were looking at a map showing seven mine locations.

'They must be hundreds of kilometres apart!' said Brooke. 'How are you going to work out which one Lear is heading to?'

Jackson leaned forward and touched the icon for one of the mines. A picture of a huge man-made hole in the ground appeared. The accompanying text said that the mine was one of the world's biggest diamond mines and was owned and operated by the De Beers Group. Jackson clicked on the company's name and a web page, with a big diamond logo, loaded. Brooke and Jackson scoured the page for anything that might catch their attention, before deciding to move on to the next mine.

Jackson's arms and legs throbbed with tiredness, and pain was radiating out from his forehead in fresh waves. Even Brooke, who was usually inexhaustible, was showing signs of wilting. They had painstakingly checked the details of five mines, and were still no closer to anything like a firm destination for Lear, when something caught Jackson's attention.

The page detailing mine number six, Duovik Diamond Mine, featured a small picture of a group of mineworkers standing with a Japanese businessman in an expensive-looking fur coat, suit and hard hat. The wording at the bottom of the text read: 'Our engineers meet Duovik's owner, Mr Yakimoto.'

Brooke would have moved on to mine number seven if Jackson hadn't gone so deathly quiet. He'd never seen an actual photograph of the man he now saw standing with his workers, but he recognized him instantly. It was Yakimoto – just as his mother had drawn him in her diary.

He peered more closely at the rawboned face in the computer monitor, searching the dark-blue round spectacles for the eyes of his mother's killer.

CHAPTER 21

'So, let me get this straight!' said Brooke, grinding the manual gears on Mr Zeal's borrowed 1970 Mark II Mini so badly that it made Jackson cringe. 'Lear is working with the guy who murdered your mother and father?'

'That's about the size of it,' Jackson replied.

'Wow! That's heavy!' said Brooke. 'I'm sorry for trying to make you talk about it the other day.'

'That's OK,' Jackson reassured her. 'But that's exactly why we must go after Lear!'

'No way, José!' The Mini swerved a little as Brooke turned to scowl at Jackson. 'Listen, I told you already, I only suggested we get Salty to pick us up so we can hide out on the island and buy us some thinkin' time. Not so you can use his boat to go to Canada on some suicide mission. As soon as we've got our evidence straight, I plan on showin' it to the authorities – and that is that!'

'Would those be the same authorities who have your dad in jail and are hoping we'll soon be joining him? All I'm saying, Brooke, is that the only way you can be sure

of us and your dad escaping jail sentences is by present-
ing the police with indisputable proof that Lear is alive
and well. The only way I can see of doing that is with
video footage of him selling reactor-irradiated diamonds
to Yakimoto.'

Brooke paused to think.

'OK. Suppose we did find a way to get you to Yakimoto's mine in Canada – which, by the way, would involve a
treacherous journey by sea, followed by a punishing drive
across some of the most challenging terrain on the planet
– what makes you think the dude is even going to be there?'

'This!' Jackson held up his phone. An email glimmered
in the centre of its glossy surface.

The Kojima twins' email response to Jackson's request
for help to find out about Yakimoto had arrived two days
ago. Jackson's recovery from the kidnapping, and their
fleeing the scene of a dirty-bomb explosion, meant that
he had only been able to check his mail and open it last
night, after Brooke had gone to sleep.

In the email, Miss Kojima said that they had given the
job of inquiring after Yakimoto to their father's head of
security. He had uncovered information about Yakimoto's business dealings, and a series of allegations that he
was involved with Japan's criminal underground.

'But, most interestingly,' Jackson told Brooke excitedly, 'he's about to fly to Canada. The twins' security guy
got the information from a private jet charter company

– Yakimoto is scheduled to take a flight from Tokyo to Calgary in Canada, in two days' time. From there, it's a quick helicopter ride to his diamond mine.'

As the Mini followed the freeway out of Boston and headed towards the coast, the fact that Brooke was no longer protesting made Jackson think his Canadian plan had a chance.

What few windows there were in Salty's cluttered boat-house, on the island of Martha's Vineyard, were either shrouded in cobwebs or obscured by the rotting bits of hull and rough wooden planks that lined the walls.

It was midday. Brooke was out on the water with Salty, but Jackson had stayed, working by the flickering light of a single faulty fluorescent strip.

What he and Brooke hadn't managed to grab from the lab during their speedy exit yesterday, they'd borrowed from Mr Zeal's apartment – some food, a pair of walking boots and a few items of cold weather clothing – the island and New England were fresh this time of year, but where he was going, just a few hundred kilometres south of the Arctic Circle, it would be considerably colder.

Brooke, having finally given in to Jackson's plan of making the trip to Canada, had even scrounged a snow chain from Salty to put round *Tread*; in Jackson's opinion, it was overkill, but he had packed it anyway.

He put the finishing touches to a battery circuit for the

satellite Internet transceiver and stuffed it into a holdall. Now Brooke too would have remote access to the robots he was planning to take with him to the wilds of Canada. He stuffed several other gadgets into the waterproof bag, including extra batteries and two of Brooke's prototype handsets in addition to the one in his shirt pocket.

Jackson and Brooke had discussed the mission's technical requirements in great detail. Jackson had been convinced that *Tread*'s gyro-stabilized high-definition cameras were ideal for the job of snooping on their targets. Brooke, however, had an even better idea.

The hoarse chug from the old fisherman's ancient trawler announced the return of Brooke and Salty. All Brooke had said, when she'd ordered her old friend to follow her several hours ago, was that she had something she needed to salvage.

Jackson believed he knew what Brooke was planning and when he saw her standing on the rusty deck of the boat, with a triumphant smile across her face, his suspicions were confirmed – silhouetted against a brooding midday sky was the glistening outline of *Punk*, a matted mane of seaweed dangling from his spikes as he swung beneath a winch.

As *Punk* was brought back to the boathouse and the three of them set to work, Brooke explained that *Verne* had made short work of recovering *Punk*.

'He might be in jail,' Salty joked, 'but J.P. will be tickled pink to know that *Verne* passed his naval salvage test!'

Luckily, Brooke had managed to bag almost all of the required hardware needed to raise *Punk* from the dead from the lab before they had left – the rest she salvaged from the junk Salty had lying around his workshop. Amazingly, the robot's main motherboard and core-processing units had survived, chiefly because of the ballistic casing in which they were sealed. Several of the tiny actuators that powered *Punk*'s moving parts had fused, and salt water had caused the hybrid turbine that powered his rotor blades to oxidize. But, even after a week on the seabed, *Punk*'s plastic ducted-fan propulsion system needed little more than drying out.

While Jackson fitted new power cells and brand-new solid-state flash drives, Salty got busy with *Punk*'s steel shell, hammering out several crumples where the metal had buckled under the immense pressure of the Great White's crushing jaws, and welding the spots where razor-sharp teeth had actually penetrated the metal.

Finally, Jackson installed *Punk*'s Linux-based operating system and the recently developed language engine.

'I think you should do the honours,' said Jackson.

'Thank you,' said Brooke, taking her phone from her pocket and punching in *Punk*'s access code and a brief message.

For a while nobody spoke, then a dim blue light pulsed behind *Punk*'s dark plastic screen, the first sign of life.

Brooke felt her handset warm slightly. She glanced at its surface. There was an SMS waiting. The message from *Punk* read: 'WAZUP?'

That evening Salty had said that the tide would be right for his and Jackson's journey northwards at around 2 a.m. the next day, so Brooke had suggested she and Jackson take a walk along the beach to fill the time.

A brisk breeze was steadily rolling in off the calm dark-grey sea, as the two of them walked the half-mile crescent of sand and pebbles.

'Turnin' into a hobby of ours, chasin' Lear!' Brooke quipped. 'Last few days, things have been moving pretty darn quick. I know it seems like we're committed to this plan to catch Lear and Yakimoto red-handed, but we can still give ourselves up, you know. We tell the Feds what we know and let them chase down the bad guys.'

'Brooke, everyone but us thinks that Lear is dead,' said Jackson. 'It's our robots on the reactor CCTV footage and us in *Tin Lizzie* leaving the scene of the explosion. What are they going to believe – that the ghost of a dead man attacked the reactor? Or a mad scientist with a grudge, who they can already connect to video evidence?'

'But that's not why you're dead set on going to Canada – is it, Jackson?'

Jackson gave a sad smile. His friend knew him better than nearly anybody. Brooke was right. It wasn't just the moral victory of showing the world that Lear was still alive and seeing him locked away for good. Or even getting J.P. out of custody – although Jackson desperately wanted that for Brooke. Canada felt like the place he might finally sort out the mystery that was his mother's life – and therefore his.

Jackson realized that they had reached the end of the beach and had started up a steep path that pointed towards a grassy headland.

'This is the way to the reservation – the whole peninsula from this point is owned by American Indians,' said Brooke. 'We can pay them a visit if you like.'

'Have we got time?' Jackson asked.

'There's time,' Brooke smiled.

They picked their way up the sandy path, Brooke leading the way to a short stretch of road, which terminated in what looked to Jackson like a plain old trailer park.

'Are you sure we've got the right place?' Jackson inquired.

'Why so?'

'Dunno. I guess I was expecting tepees and totem poles!'

Brooke laughed as she marched up to a long silver trailer and banged at the door.

The door swung open immediately, and a very large man wearing a cowboy hat and red plaid shirt stood in the doorway. 'Brooke!' he shouted when he caught sight of her.

'Hi, Chief!' said Brooke as the enormous man scooped her up in a bear hug.

'Are ya here with the prof?'

'Er, no . . . Dad's busy . . .' said Brooke, throwing a glance in Jackson's direction.

Salty obviously hadn't passed this news from the mainland on to his island neighbour. Jackson noticed there was no TV or radio either.

'We hiked up here. Jackson, this is John Appleseed, otherwise known as Eagle Chief!'

'Make yourselves comfortable,' said the man, beckoning them inside.

If Jackson had been disappointed by the lack of anything he considered obviously *Indian* outside, the trailer's interior was another matter – memorabilia and artefacts were everywhere, a huge black-and-white feather headdress fanned out across the wall and, below it, a collection of sepia photographs featuring American Indian families and proud old warriors with dark, leathery faces. The other wall held a cluster of hand-knapped flint knives and tomahawks with wound-leather handles and, beyond that, more photographs lined the corridor.

'John is the third descendant of the original Eagle Chief of the Wampanoag Indians,' Brooke told Jackson.

'This is him,' the chief said, pointing at a black-and-white photograph in the centre of the wall, which featured an elderly man with long, thick braids of black hair beneath an elaborate war headdress. Jackson looked at the photograph of the old man. His chin was slightly raised and he was staring intently out of the picture frame with a serious expression. Jackson thought he looked every bit the warrior chief.

'So, Jackson,' the chief said, taking his cowboy hat off and running his fingers through a thick head of long jet-black hair, 'what brings an Englishman to New England?'

'I'm studying at the university, on a scholarship with J.P.,' replied Jackson.

'Then you must be a very clever young man. J.P. only works with the best,' said the chief.

Jackson nodded but, in his mind, the idea of attending lectures and doing homework belonged to a dim and distant past.

'Is everything OK, Brooke?' continued the chief. 'It's quite late for a visit!'

'Everything's cool,' she said calmly. 'Jackson is going on an expedition tomorrow and I wondered if you had a travel charm.'

The chief smiled and moved over into the corner of the room, where the kitchen was. As he spoke, he poured tea into three small cups, from a large pot on the stove.

'You should know better, Brooke. Charms are for tourists – something they can put round their necks to show their friends that they met the Indians.' The chief raised his eyebrows in mock amazement. 'Are you a tourist,

Jackson?' He smiled as he handed Jackson a cup of hot, black tea.

'No,' said Jackson firmly.

The chief turned his attention back to Brooke. 'Then my guess is that this journey is a dangerous one!'

'Kinda,' Brooke replied.

The chief didn't question Brooke any further but looked at Jackson inquisitively, as if he was sizing up whether or not he was worthy of his help. He got up and walked over to a large wooden chest and opened it. 'My ancestors believed that each journey they took ended in two different locations, a place for their body, and a place for their soul.' He pulled a colourful bead necklace from the chest, along with an old leatherbound book. Then he walked back to the sofa and, motioning to Jackson to lean forward, placed the necklace over his head.

'Before a member of the tribe undertook a perilous journey, he first shared sustenance with the chief and his family.' Eagle Chief took Jackson's cup from his hand, drank from it and handed it to Brooke, who did the same.

'And finally,' said the chief, his pale-blue eyes staring right at Jackson's. 'He asked the gods that this trip bring him closer to an understanding of the true nature of his life's journey.'

Eagle Chief handed Jackson the old book. 'Open it, at whatever page you like. According to my ancestors, the true nature of your journey will reveal itself to you.'

The notion that arbitrary pages from the chief's book could tell Jackson anything he really needed to know didn't tally with his scientific brain, but Jackson didn't want to be rude to the chief.

Feeling a little self-conscious, Jackson let his thumbs part the book around two thirds in. The text was a meticulous calligraphy in faded black ink, but a few words in and the words behind the fancy, swirly font became clear.

All things in the world are two.
Strong and weak, wise and unwise,
Friend and foe, father and son.
With our eyes we see two things,
Things that are fair and things that are ugly.
One foot may lead us to the right way,
The other foot may lead us down a different path.
So are all things two, always two.

Brooke talked the whole way back to Salty's, but Jackson remained quiet. He wasn't sure how, or even why, but the ancient book's words had really seemed to relate to the things he was going through. Even so, as they left the beach and climbed up to the boathouse, Jackson decided that thoughts of Indian wisdom would have to wait – it was time he set out on the trail of the men who haunted him.

CHAPTER 22

An overpowering feeling of nausea woke Jackson.

He was drunk with tiredness, but forced himself to get up and run to the metal steps that led out on to the deck of the trawler before hurling a stomachful of vomit over the side.

The sun was up, but it was bitterly cold. Jackson stood in his T-shirt and jeans, shivering, trying to detect the signs of a second round of seasickness, when he noticed the thin strip of land beside them.

'Bonjour, Canada!' It was Salty and he had a thick, fur-lined coat that he placed over Jackson's shoulders.

'Coastguard brought his launch alongside us, while you was sleepin'. Gave us a right good scour with his spotlight. Dare say he thought that a runaway international terrorist, such as yourself, would put his nose up at a smelly old bag o' bones like her ladyship.' Salty lovingly patted the handrail like it was a dog.

International terrorist? thought Jackson. He had to

admit it, though, he was living the lifestyle – stowed away in the middle of the ocean.

But at least he felt as if he was taking action against Lear and Yakimoto. He didn't envy Brooke. They'd been so busy getting the kit for the mission together that Jackson hadn't had a chance to discuss with her where she was going to hide out. It would need to be somewhere the police would never think of looking. There had never been any doubt that Brooke would stay behind, even though she couldn't allow herself to be seen by anyone – she wanted to remain close to Boston where she could keep up with developments in her father's case.

Time aboard the trawler dragged. Jackson had checked and re-checked the kit, making sure batteries were charged and transmitting refinements to the route he and Brooke had chosen. Aside from a period of about twenty minutes when the boat was followed by dolphins, the journey was tediously uneventful.

A thick canopy of cloud was waiting for Jackson and Salty as they left the Atlantic behind and navigated the desolate corridor of water that led into the Hudson Bay. As they approached the port of Cape Churchill, it was as if a heavy white curtain had been drawn all around them. Jackson stayed outside as long as he could stand it, preferring the freezing snowflakes to the musty lower deck. It was a wonder to him how Salty found his way into Churchill's seaport at all, given they were now in total white-out.

With the trawler tied up, Salty helped Jackson carry his cases off the boat and hide them under some tarpaulin. Then, with a firm handshake, he was gone.

Jackson pulled the fur-lined hood of his coat up round his face to keep out the bitterly cold driving snow, then set off in search of his next ride.

'Goddamit!' shouted Brooke.

As she lifted the hot dog out of the flames of her fire, both bread and sausage were indistinguishable from charcoal. *Next time*, she thought, *I'll try cooking them separately.*

Technologically, Brooke's camp was on a par with some high-tech military installations – she might be sleeping in a tepee in hills above her house on Martha's Vineyard, but she was sharing the bandwidth of a conveniently located Wi-Fi Max ultra high-speed Internet transmitter. The cable she'd managed to run from a wind turbine substation was supplying all the electricity she needed for her computers, her 60-inch LED flatscreen and the electric bike and trailer she'd used to transport it all up the hill from her boathouse.

Brooke's tablet computer screen flashed with an incoming video call.

'So tell me the good news,' said Brooke. 'You in Canada yet?'

'Yes,' Jackson replied. 'And I think I've found a vehicle.'

'What is it?' inquired Brooke excitedly.

Jackson held his phone up to the vehicle he was standing next to.

'A snowplough!' said Brooke gleefully. 'I'd say it's a converted Ford dump truck, by the looks of the chassis.'

Jackson was pleased his choice obviously met with Brooke's expert approval. He'd picked this vehicle from several different cars and trucks parked in an enclosure because the cabin was high enough to hide him from the drivers of most other cars and because, judging by the snow sweeping across the harbour in thick waves, he might need the robust truck. And there was the small matter that it was the only vehicle in the lot that wasn't locked!

'Pop the hood!' said Brooke. 'The lever is probably located underneath the steering wheel.'

Jackson climbed up into the truck's cabin and pulled a large rubberized handle under the dashboard.

With Brooke's instructions coming from his phone's directional speaker, Jackson worked on the engine in blizzard conditions. He'd packed gloves for the trip, but rewiring the engine's electrics required all the dexterity of his bare fingers. To his great relief, the components that gave Brooke's robotic Chauffeur its senses – the sonar, infrared and Ultra-HD video transmitters – were fully wireless. Thanks to powerful magnets, they stuck easily to the roof, bonnet and boot and, most ingeniously, induced the electric current they required through the truck's metal bodywork.

Whenever they sensed road markings, signs, other cars or pedestrians with a death wish, they would communicate via radio waves with the Chauffeur's tablet computer brain, which Jackson had taped to the dashboard. With the satellite transceiver mounted securely on the roof, to keep Brooke and Jackson connected when their phones lost signal, Jackson could finally get out of the cold.

Next, Brooke guided him in the installation of three metal actuators, one that attached to the steering wheel, one to the transmission lever and one to the foot pedals.

The whole operation took about an hour, but even in that time the snow had started to build up around the wheels and radiators of the other vehicles in the pound and Jackson was keen to get going.

'Ready for start up?' said Jackson.

'Almost there! Just waiting for your satellite dish to get a lock.'

There was a momentary pause before Brooke came back.

'OK, that's locked and loaded! Because of the mountains your dish might lose its connection for a minute or two. It'll sort itself out eventually, but there will be patches where the signal between us will break up. Right, Jacko, you ready to roll?'

'I'd say so! You want to do the honours or shall I?' Jackson asked.

'Ladies first!' said Brooke.

Jackson was looking at the screen of the slimline tablet computer when the virtual button IGNITION depressed itself. He was flushed with a mixture of relief and trepidation as the diesel engine coughed into life without any manual assistance from him whatsoever. A second later and the metal arm Jackson had fixed to the transmission lever slid the gear stick into DRIVE and the truck trundled forward.

'Go easy, Brooke, this weather is atrocious,' Jackson implored as the six-tonne snowplough built up speed.

'It's not me you should be telling about back-seat driving – the old gal's driving herself!'

'Is that supposed to make me feel better?' asked Jackson.

'Don't worry too much; she can drive blind if she needs to. Take a look at your screen and you'll see what your truck is seeing!'

Jackson glanced at the tablet screen, and the almost solid white of the view forwards suddenly flicked to something that resembled a watercolour painting of the environment around the car. Lurid reds, blues and purples were daubed on to the outlines of the vehicles, buildings, intersections and road signs; it was a three-dimensional rendering of what the sonar and infrared sensors were seeing.

'All I'll say is to look out for the reds!' said Brooke. 'The Chauffeur's computer paints red anything it perceives as dangerous. If you get too close to a kerb, it'll appear in red. If a kid wanders into the road – red! That's when you'll need to hold on, as the Chauffeur system's Collision Avoidance will kick in.'

'OK,' said Jackson. 'And you've programmed in the route?'

'Sure have. You'll join a highway in around...' Brooke paused to check her computer screen. 'Fifty-two minutes! It will eventually lead you into Yellowknife.'

'Canada's diamond capital,' murmured Jackson.

'You betcha! From there it's a short hop northwards, on the ice road!'

The ice road, thought Jackson. At any other time, it would have sounded really cool, if only he didn't actually have to drive on it.

The snow didn't let up, as the self-driving truck ate up hundreds of kilometres of frozen roads.

Jackson had stopped once to pick up fuel and a plastic sandwich, and hadn't passed a single other vehicle since.

All he could make out through the windows of the truck were the sawblade edges of pine forests and the odd glint of a road sign as it flashed past. It was easier to concentrate on this than the questions in his head about his mum. He sighed. One thing he did feel sure of was that his only chance of finding answers lay at the end of these endless snow-covered roads.

CHAPTER 23

'Jackson!' shouted Brooke. 'Jackson, wake up! You've reached Yellowknife!'

Jackson peeled his face from the plastic armrest. He looked at the clock on the dashboard – 5.30 a.m. 'Good job,' he said. 'According to the Kojima twins, Yakimoto's jet is due to land in Calgary about now. I can't waste any time.'

Outside the truck, it was still snowing, but not as hard as it had been during the night. The truck was rolling down the wide high street, freshly laid snow creaking as it compacted beneath its fat tyres. The sun glowed a soft orange, but Jackson didn't bank on it getting much brighter today.

Soon Yellowknife vanished in the truck's wake, all traces of civilization – even the road markings – gone. All that distinguished the path to the North-west Territories were verges made of chunks of ice and rock.

'Looks kinda barren, don't it?' commented Brooke, looking at the featureless terrain in boxes on her tablet touchscreen, which were fed by the truck's wireless cameras.

'It looks cold,' replied Jackson.

Suddenly there was a loud beeping sound.

Jackson checked the display of his tablet computer – straight across the strip of blue that represented the road was a thick, pulsating band of red. No sooner had Jackson been notified of the threat than the actuator that controlled the brake pedal began to hiss, and the rod that ran down its centre shot forward. It was the Chauffeur's Collision Avoidance system.

The truck started to slide, in a straight line at first – then it began to slowly revolve. In any other situation, the Collision Avoidance system's emergency braking would have saved Jackson, but not here – not on an ice road!

With the wheels still locked, the vehicle had almost completed a full revolution when Jackson saw what it was that the automated driving computer was trying to avoid; about fifty metres ahead of him, a chunk of road, as wide as an Olympic swimming pool, had been eaten away by a fast-flowing river.

Jackson wasted no time – he grabbed the steering wheel and prepared to take control. 'Brooke!' he bellowed. 'I need a manual override – and I need it quick!'

But there was no answer.

Jackson shouted her name again, before the penny dropped. It was what she'd told him to expect – *patches where the signal between us will break up*. He was in the middle of nowhere – there was no Brooke and no way of disengaging the robotic driver, intent on killing him.

The truck slammed into the rocky river bed and the galvanized steel plough blade it carried on the front buried itself, bonnet deep, in ice and silt. Jackson was thrown forward, smashing his head on the centre of the steering wheel.

The last sensations Jackson felt, before he slipped into unconsciousness, were of freezing cold water rising up his leg and the metallic taste of blood.

Jackson shook himself awake. His whole body was shaking involuntarily as the icy water, which had now reached his waist, had dropped his core temperature to dangerously low levels.

His head was pounding and the impact from the crash had opened up his forehead wound again. Jackson looked at the clump of broken stitches in the truck's cracked mirror. Lear's surgical handiwork was ruined. *Good!* he thought – it wouldn't kill him. However, the icy water would and Jackson knew he had to get out – and quickly.

He unclipped his seat belt and tried to open the door. But it was no good; there was no way he could compete with the force of the rushing water. Jackson dipped his hand below the level of the freezing water and found the handle to the window.

With the window rolled down, he was able to climb out into the thrusting current of the river, but even then he couldn't just make for the relative safety of the fractured road that lay a metre above him, because if he was to survive at all, let alone continue his journey to the mine, he needed the gear he'd packed – warm clothes, food and the robots.

Jackson retrieved the twisted satellite dish, which hung from the truck's roof by a cable. With no cellular towers for miles, which his handset needed to work long distance, and with the satellite link busted, he wouldn't be talking to Brooke any time soon.

It took all of Jackson's strength to drag two of the cases from the back of the cabin out through the window and push them up on to the road. *Tread* would be too heavy to lift up to the road, so Jackson just dragged him into the water, and floated him a short way downstream, where, with his last dregs of energy, he was able to roll the robot on to the frozen river bank.

As he lay there, his throat burning from his attempts to drag down much needed oxygen, Jackson was aware that he couldn't rest. The snow hadn't abated, and now that he was outside a stiff wind pulled at his wet clothes. He rolled over and his frozen fingers fumbled to unzip one of the bags. Inside were the clothes he'd brought from Mr Zeal's apartment and the coat Salty had lent him.

Even with the dry clothes on, Jackson continued to

shiver uncontrollably. His gloved hands were still numb and, despite Zeal's dry boots, his feet were blocks of ice. He was no doctor, but Jackson knew that being this cold, in a place like this, could soon lead to frostbite and hypothermia.

Jackson limped towards the bags he'd swung on to the road and found the one in which he'd packed *Punk*. He rolled the robot on to the road, then groped painfully in his breast pocket for his phone; one of the advantages of the handset's sealed plastic slab design was that it was one-hundred-per-cent waterproof. Every stroke and gesture with the phone was painful, but slowly Jackson was able to initiate *Punk*'s start-up procedure.

Punk wobbled as his twelve spikes shot out and steadied him against the rocks. Using a test program Brooke had designed to calibrate *Punk*'s ducted fans, Jackson set their thrust to two per cent. The robot rattled against the rocks as the tiny engines spooled up. Jackson wasted no time and curled his body round the machine, trying his best to avoid being poked by the spikes. It was a relief when the warm air thrusting from *Punk*'s vents started to flow into Jackson's trousers and jacket.

It only took about twenty minutes for him to feel stronger – twenty minutes in which he also managed to think of a possible way to get out of the freezing blizzard he was now facing, without even a truck or shelter, and on to Yakimoto's mine.

Jackson didn't waste time taking *Fist* out of his bag; he just started him up and let him rip himself out. It took several trial-and-error gestures to get *Fist* into the shape Jackson had in mind – but, eventually, his four large plastic hands were cupped in a shape that resembled a cradle.

Jackson had his dogsled – now he needed a dog!

He accessed *Tread*'s defence systems menu and selected the stinger. Being careful to point the robotic wheel's right-side chrome hub away from himself, he fired the lightweight toughened-nylon strip. The five-metre strip shot out across the road, some of its titanium barbs biting into the ice, while others sat upright, ready to rip open the tyres of unsuspecting runaway cars.

Jackson grabbed the end of the strip and walked it back to *Tread*, looping it around the gyro-stabilized camera that sat in the centre of the hub on the other side of the wheel. Then he carefully knotted the nylon strip round the camera housing, its sharp barbs helping to secure it.

Finally, Jackson salvaged what tech he needed from the bags and loaded it on to *Fist*, along with himself and *Punk*.

Moments later and the snow squall was stinging his face. But Jackson didn't care – he was belting northwards along the ice road at 60 kilometres an hour.

CHAPTER 24

Jackson's makeshift sledge sped along the ice road – one of *Fist*'s super-smooth and ultra-robust plastic hands holding the nylon reins, the rest acting as runners. Thanks to the snow chain he was wearing, *Tread* was making short work of the ice and rock, and after only an hour of bone shaking and extreme cold it looked as if Jackson's thrill ride might finally be at an end.

Through the windblown snow, he caught sight of the blurry outline of a compound.

Jackson dialled down the throttle setting of *Tread*'s electric motor so he could glide closer for a better look. A tall fence that seemed to stretch across the entire visible horizon came slowly into focus, and then a large red sign:

DUOVIK DIAMOND MINE
Private Property
No Unauthorized Access!
Trespassers will be met with lethal force.

Jackson climbed from *Fist* and stretched his aching limbs. He was battered, bruised and exhausted from the effort it had taken just to hold on to his improvised sledge, and the thought of entering the lion's den filled him with trepidation. He was tired and the wound on his head was throbbing, but at the same time he knew this was the only chance he had to catch Lear and Yakimoto red-handed. All J.P. had ever done was help him, and now he was locked up. The only sure way Jackson knew of changing that situation, and avenging the deaths of his parents, lay beyond the fence.

Jackson thought he could pick out voices, carried by the strong gusts of wind coming from the east. They were coming from where he suspected the road led into the compound. It was logical that there would be guards stationed there. He couldn't risk trying to find an unmanned gate. *If I can't find a way round the fence*, he thought grimly, *I'll just have to go through it!*

Jackson punched up *Fist*. The robot's industrial-strength memory metal muscles hardly needed to flex at all in order to prise open a hole in the fence, big enough for Jackson and his kit.

Brooke didn't do patient.

It had been two anxious hours since her connection to Jackson had been severed. She'd expected the communications link between them to re-establish itself within minutes. But after almost two hours all she had on her touchscreen was static.

For all she knew, Jackson was lying dead in a frozen ditch.

To make matters worse, she had come up with the idea of accessing the IP address of the security camera system her dad used to monitor their Martha's Vineyard house from the mainland. She could only watch, infuriated, as FBI agents rifled through her stuff. It was a good job that Jackson had the robots with him, otherwise Brooke might not have been able to resist sending *Punk* and *Fist* down the valley to kick them out of her place.

She'd even begun to question the logic of their evading capture. She allowed herself to picture her father in the police cell. While she was on the run, there was no way she could risk letting him know she was OK. He'd be sick with worry. The familiar sting of guilt was back. This was all her fault. If she wasn't such a thrill seeker, she'd never have got caught up with MeX in the first place. It seemed that everything she built got her and her dad into trouble. She'd almost killed herself in *Tin Lizzie*, caused havoc with *Fist* and blown up most parts of the lab with various experiments. And the person it always seemed to hurt was her dad.

She really did *suck* in the daughter department.

When the Messenger software on her screen finally flashed, showing an incoming message from Jackson, she couldn't answer it fast enough.

'What happened to you?' she said, her voice charged with relief.

'The snowplough decided to go for a swim,' replied Jackson.

Brooke was horrified. 'Are you OK?' she asked.

'I'm all right, but I think you'll need to find a new Chauffeur.'

'To hell with that! Where are you? It's not too late to call this off, Jackson!' Her voice was frightened.

'It's all right, Brooke,' said Jackson. 'Everything is under control.'

Jackson glanced around. He had scrabbled inside some kind of storehouse and immediately set about fixing the broken satellite dish before venturing back outside to secure it to the side of the building. He'd magnetically clicked together all three of the phones he had brought with him to form a narrow crescent-shaped widescreen, which he'd propped up on an oil drum. The view was showing him the compound via several of *Punk*'s cameras. In one of the video boxes, Jackson could see a large Sikorsky Executive Transport Helicopter sitting on a helipad.

'You should be receiving *Punk*'s feed now,' said Jackson. 'I'm guessing Yakimoto has recently arrived. If you switch to the thermal view, you can see there's no one in the helicopter, but its turbine is still warm.'

Brooke followed Jackson's instructions and she could clearly see the hot red outline of a jet turbine engine in the top section of the helicopter – meaning it had only landed a short time ago.

'Any sign of Lear?'

'Not yet! But the mine is big. Really big.'

Jackson rotated his phone hand. Instantly, the main view from *Punk* pivoted until a cavernous pit appeared through the snow flurry. Jackson had to pan *Punk*'s view in order to see the entirety of the immense hole in the ground.

'*Punk*'s done a quick thermal sweep of the buildings near me, and the only other people up here look to be two security men guarding the main entrance.'

'So Yakimoto's down there,' said Brooke, poking the screen of her tablet computer. A reciprocal marker, representing where Brooke had placed her finger, appeared in the centre of the mine on Jackson's display.

'Mind if I go manual for this one?' asked Brooke enthusiastically.

'Be my guest!' replied Jackson.

On Brooke's direction, *Punk* crested the snaggy edge of the mine hole. The scale of the excavation was breathtaking – it looked so wide and deep that Jackson imagined it could swallow up an entire city. Around the edge, a thread of pathways, gnawed out by machines, corkscrewed downwards around the sheer walls of rock and ice.

The metal robot tracked the frozen path, descending through clouds of swirling snow as his cameras struggled to focus through the milky haze. Eventually, Brooke and Jackson saw the dim glow of a tunnel and Brooke directed her spiked spy towards it.

The tunnel was illuminated by a series of electric lanterns hanging from the ceiling. As he hovered by the cave entrance, *Punk*'s video showed uniform bite marks on the rock surface, made by the drilling machine that had scooped the cave out.

Punk flew slowly down the passageway, then, rounding a corner, came across a large open chamber. The underground cave was high enough to house a huge drilling machine and a small crane on tracks. Most intriguing of all were four white loaders parked in a line.

'What are those?' asked Jackson.

'D'you what? I don't know,' came Brooke's puzzled reply.

It was the first time, in Jackson's experience, that the identity of a vehicle had eluded Brooke. Thanks to her life-long love affair with machinery of every description, Brooke had an uncanny ability to spot the telltale chassis configuration, axle arrangement or load-lifting faculty of even the most exotic industrial contraption. The fact that these three loaders were unregistered in the red-haired mechanic's mental database made them quite extraordinary.

As *Punk* swept slowly along the line of shiny white machines, Jackson thought they had the appearance of bi-pedal robots – a large glass half-sphere for a head, powerful metal shoulders and arms with vice-like pinchers for hands and two stout metal legs.

'They're powerlifters!' said Brooke. 'It makes sense – the Japanese have been working on this technology for years. A worker climbs inside and the robotic exoskeleton around him gives him the lifting ability of a forklift truck.'

The stereoscopic audio sensor in one of *Punk*'s spikes momentarily peaked and Brooke and Jackson's attention was drawn to the sound of talking. Four men were walking towards the line of lifters near the spot where *Punk* was loitering. Brooke swished her handset in three precise patterns, which directed *Punk* to shoot between the legs of one of the lifters.

From his position on the ground, one of *Punk*'s cameras could still see the backs of the four men as they stood talking. It was hard to see any distinguishing features, but two of the men were larger than the others, their broad shoulders obvious even through their thick coats. *Bodyguards*, thought Jackson.

One of the men turned and held something up to the light in the ceiling.

Brooke touched her display in order to guide *Punk*'s focus and a shiny rock, about the size of a plum, flashed from the end of the man's fingers.

'A diamond in the rough!' said Brooke.

But Jackson wasn't looking at the stone; his attention was on the man holding it. It was Yakimoto.

It was amazing to Jackson how the face of the real Yakimoto evoked his mother's drawing. There was the photograph from the Internet of him standing with the mineworkers – but it was his mother's doodle that accentuated the blades of his cheekbones and the thick, flowing jet-black hair. He was even wearing the blue round spectacles from his mother's sketch, pushed up on his forehead as he inspected the stone with his naked eye.

'Are you getting this on hard disk?' he whispered, not wanting even the vibration of his own voice to spoil the clarity of the moment.

'Safe and sound, cuz!' Brooke responded.

'What are they saying?'

'It's just coming through now . . .'

Brooke had carefully repositioned *Punk* so his listening spike could better tune in to what the men were saying. Slowly, fragments of conversation came through the speakers built into Brooke's and Jackson's respective devices.

'Quite extraordinary, Mr Botha,' said Yakimoto.

'Thank you, sir,' said the shortest and fattest of the four men, in between coughs.

'And this is the twenty-seventh gemstone of this carat and colour you've found in my mine?'

'Yes, all the stones were uncovered in the same cavity of the Kimberlite pipe. We've roughly polished several of them and they are all the same exquisite blue colour.'

'Naturally occurring blue topaz diamonds like these, Botha, are extremely rare!' Yakimoto exuberantly stated. 'Why are the men who found them not here? I want to congratulate them.'

'Charles and Dominick called in sick this morning, Mr Yakimoto, sir.' Mr Botha coughed and sniffed again. It was clear to Jackson from the small plump man's overalls, and his deferential treatment of Mr Yakimoto, that he was some kind of foreman. 'They've been working like dogs for the last two days trying to clear the pipe of all the stones, in readiness for your arrival,' the man explained.

'And you're sure you've got them all?' said Yakimoto.

'We've scanned the seam and we're confident that's it, sir.' He hacked up something and turned his head to spit it away from the group.

'Good! Well, Mr Botha,' the Japanese man said, bowing sharply in his direction, 'your team have excelled themselves. This has to be one of the greatest diamond finds of the decade. I will see to it that you and your men are handsomely rewarded. Now, I suggest we return to the office and prepare the stones for me to transport them back to Japan.'

The four men disappeared from *Punk*'s video stream for a few seconds, then reappeared in a small open-top six-wheeled all-terrain vehicle.

Brooke commanded *Punk* to follow the men up the steep path.

'Can you enlighten me as to what is going on here?' said Brooke, keeping *Punk* at a safe distance behind the men. 'I thought we were going to film Lear handing over the stolen diamonds to his partner in crime. Maybe I'm missing something, but didn't we just watch Yucky-moto being handed diamonds found in his own mine?'

'I don't understand what's going on myself,' replied Jackson. Had he and Brooke just seen the stolen diamonds? They were blue, just as Atticus79 had told him they would be after being irradiated in a nuclear reactor. So why was Yakimoto's own foreman handing him Lear's stolen diamonds as if they'd just been pulled out of the mine?

'Jackson! I'm getting a faint reading of something near your cabin!' It was Brooke. As the ATV surfaced from the mine, she spotted a shape that could be a person or perhaps a guard dog in the small video box she'd reserved for *Punk*'s thermal-imaging overlay.

Jackson's senses sharpened. He turned his head to see if he could spot anything through the window. Nothing. He crept across the room and opened a crack in the door. The freezing blast was shocking – it was amazing how, in such a short space of time, Jackson had already grown accustomed to the warmth of the small gas fire inside the building where he was hiding. He didn't relish the thought of venturing outside again.

'From what I can see, there's no one out there, Brooke.'

'Nope. I'm definitely seeing a trace of something or

someone. It's hard to say, but I'm guessing they are now behind your cabin.'

Once again Jackson walked to the door and pushed it slightly ajar. At the same time, the image of a warm mass on Brooke's screen vanished.

'Well, that's weird!' she said. 'Perhaps *Punk*'s still got some sea water sloshing around inside his circuits!' But even as she spoke, the apparition, a blob of purplish-red rather than the identifiable shapes Brooke was used to seeing, reappeared.

'I'm sorry,' said Brooke quietly and slowly. 'Either I didn't pick up something when I ran the diagnostics for *Punk*'s thermal processor – or something is stalking you!'

A shiver ran down Jackson's spine, and it wasn't because of the cold. 'You stay on Yakimoto,' he whispered. 'I guess I'll have to investigate outside.'

Jackson couldn't risk attracting the attention of the guards – so he made sure *Tread* was in stealth mode as he slowly opened the door to his storeroom and let him out.

'Where's the signal now?' Jackson asked.

'It's crazy, Jackson. It just vanished – the second you opened the door!' replied Brooke.

'I'll let *Tread* off his leash for a bit. If there is someone creeping around outside, I'd rather know about it!'

Jackson used his phone to weave *Tread* steadily through the ground-level complex. The wheel-bot passed the accommodation block and two corrugated-metal structures that housed an assortment of vehicles, including a line of three more of the white powerlifters Brooke and Jackson had spotted in the mine. Despite the driving snow, *Tread*'s UHD camera fed crisp images back to Jackson's widescreen display, now made up of two handsets. As he rounded the garage area, *Tread* offered a gyroscopically level shot of the two guards in the hut near the gate. A moment later Yakimoto and the other men entered the shot in their ATV, and then left again as they entered a hut.

With *Tread*'s tour of the buildings over, Jackson had to conclude that Brooke might have been right about the water in *Punk*'s sensors. He was about to let her know all looked OK when a small object flashed quickly across his display.

It appeared and disappeared so quickly that it made Jackson jump.

'There, in front of *Tread*! Did you see it?' snapped Jackson.

Through *Punk*'s thermal camera feed Brooke could see the shape of *Tread* clearly, his warm electric engine glowing at his core. But the only other heat signatures in the camp were Yakimoto's group and the two gatekeepers.

'I'm seeing nothing, Jackson,' she said.

'Wait a minute!' He had an idea. 'Everything *Tread* is seeing goes on to my phone's hard drive, right?'

'Yes,' replied Brooke. 'Everything *Tread* sees is stored as a video file inside him and, if there's enough bandwidth, which with your Wi-Fi Max connection there is, it is simultaneously transferred to the controlling device – that being your phone.'

Jackson swiped the surface of the phone in his hand to bring up its desktop, then navigated to video playback. As he snapped the device in various directions, the phone's gestural interface picked up the commands to open and then fast-forward the latest video file. Seconds later and Jackson drew a 'P' for PLAY in the air and the video of what *Tread* had recorded, only moments ago, started to roll.

Just as Jackson had seen it, a small blurred anomaly flashed across the screen, from right to left. Jackson quickly formed the gestural sign for PAUSE in the air and then rewound the footage frame by frame, by gently tapping the left side of the device.

To his complete amazement, with each tap, the object that had darted in front of *Tread* slowly edged into the centre of his phone's radiant surface. Hanging in the air, in the centre of the freeze-frame, could be seen not one but three identical round balls that Jackson guessed were no bigger than tennis balls in size. They appeared to be flying in perfect geometrical formation, forming the three points of an equilateral triangle.

This fragment of a second's worth of video footage confirmed Jackson's theory: Lear's robot swarm was real.

And if the swarm was here – so was Lear.

CHAPTER 25

Jackson had to laugh. Here he was in Canada's frozen wastelands where the temperature outside was enough to take his breath away – but Brooke was the one getting cold feet.

'I've got a bad feeling about this, Jackson,' said Brooke. 'If you're right and Lear is there – hunkered down outside the compound most likely – then what's to say he's not watching you right now? His swarm could attack you at any time, Jackson. I say you get out of there. We've got the conversation from the cave and you have footage of the swarm that attacked the reactor! It might be enough for Dad's lawyers.'

'*Might* isn't good enough, Brooke. We need more than that,' said Jackson, ignoring her advice. 'What's our Japanese friend up to?'

Despite the very real possibility of being shot by the guards or attacked by swarm-bots, Jackson wanted nothing more than to run out of the building in which he was hiding and into the hut where he knew Yakimoto was.

He turned over a scenario in his mind in which he could follow this urge and direct *Fist* to tear the man limb from limb. But Jackson knew that his desire for revenge threatened to spark an explosion that could lose him, Brooke and J.P. their only chance of exoneration. He forced the hatred back inside him. Yakimoto would wait. Lear was the priority for now. Footage of the world's most famous dead man would end all this.

'Jackson, you're impossible!' Brooke shouted, before reluctantly answering his question. 'They've finished packing the diamonds and are discussing business details. I doubt it'll be long before he lifts off. Visibility is bad enough and it'll be night-time soon. Which brings me to my next question. How do you intend to get out of there?'

'Don't worry about me,' he said. 'When we're ready, you can tell the FBI where I am and let them figure out how I'm getting home. In the meantime, stay on Yakimoto and I'll see if I can find where Lear is hiding.'

The streaming video from *Tread* showed the uniwheeled robot approaching the breach in the perimeter fence that *Fist* had created. Under Jackson's control, *Tread* shot through the hole and out into snow-covered terrain beyond.

Tread's tyre grabbed at the hard-packed snow as he continued his patrol. With a wide sweeping turn, he sped on towards the hazy outline of the setting sun. Jackson studied every detail of the wintery vista from *Tread*'s camera, zooming in on dubious-looking trees and rock formations.

The robot had been running as fast as the slippery uneven ground would allow, when Jackson noticed a lump on the horizon that seemed out of place. He altered *Tread*'s course to arc him round the suspect mound. It was situated another hundred metres or so out from the mine perimeter and was only visible because its 'white' was a different hue to the snow all around it. The snowfall had given the landscape beyond the mine a uniform sleekness, and now the sun was lower in the sky, everywhere was tinged with orange – except the smooth hump *Tread* was closing in on.

Jackson commanded *Tread* to slow down as he rolled round the back of the mound. There, behind a snow-camouflage cover, was an encampment, and at its centre stood an eight-wheel amphibious truck with a huge storage container on the back.

'Are you seeing this?' said Jackson.

'It's a HEMTT,' said Brooke confidently. It stands for Heavy Expanded Mobility Tactical Truck! Call it a military-grade motorhome or a luxury mobile hideaway if you're a runaway billionaire! With the generator on board that thing, Lear could stay out there for a month. It's the perfect command centre for whatever the heck he and his swarm are up to.'

This is it, thought Jackson. *Lear is in there. He has to be. But how to coax the rat out?*

'I've been thinking,' said Brooke. 'I might have figured out how all this works. Lear steals and irradiates the diamonds. Then he gets Yakimoto to legitimize them by miraculously finding the coloured gems in his mine.'

'I was thinking the same thing, Brooke,' said Jackson. 'But, if that's the case, why is Lear hiding in a camouflaged compound out here?'

Suddenly *Tread*'s video feed started to quiver, and soon the image on the surface of Jackson's dual phone screen was shaking so much it was virtually impossible for Jackson to make out Lear's camp any more. He was in the process of pulling *Tread* round to try and reorientate the robot's antennae and clear what he thought was electrical interference, when the source of the problem revealed itself. Behind *Tread*, a spinning ring of tiny tennis-ball-sized robots was hovering just above the snow.

Jackson guessed that there were about ten swarm machines making up the revolving ring, which was increasing in speed. He suspected that the interference he had seen on *Tread*'s feed was caused by the red glowing lights at the centre of each of the mini mechanical globes, which looked like some kind of laser array. Seconds later a bright red charge seemed to skip between each member of the ring-shaped swarm.

'Get *Tread* out of there!' shouted Brooke. 'If you ask me, they're spooling up to strike!'

Then, just as Jackson was beginning to drive *Tread*

backwards away from the swarm, a pulse of laser light shot from the whirling mass. *Tread* was already moving so the straight beam of light only glanced off his casing, but whatever metal was touched was cut from *Tread*'s body with the ease of a knife through butter.

'Hot diggity! What just happened?' yelled Brooke, sharing part of the spectacle on *Tread*'s camera.

'My guess is it's the same laser drill they used to get into MIT's reactor – but you're the expert!' Jackson shouted as he jackknifed *Tread* through a high-speed one-eighty and beat a hasty retreat in the direction of the compound.

'A single beam of laser light from a robot that small?' Brooke mused. 'It can only be a chemical laser of hydrogen fluoride. The beam on just one of those babies won't do much more than scorch ya. But when the swarm shares wireless energy – hooyah – you do not want to get in the way! At least now we know how they cut their way into the reactor.'

Tread was no longer in stealth mode – his engine was screaming at full revs as he ignored the hole in the fence and tore himself a new one. But as he went through it, a section of the fence snagged on some of the wiring that was hanging out of his newly cropped casing. A lead that connected to part of *Tread*'s braking system ripped out, causing his disc brake to lock. The wheel-bot careered straight into one of the corrugated buildings near Jackson.

By the time Jackson had realized what was happening,

the swarm had caught up with *Tread*. With *Tread*'s brake jammed, Jackson had little choice but to abandon control of him and turn his attention to *Fist*.

Jackson swapped the software control interface on his handset and in a microsecond *Fist* had grabbed the window sill inside the hut where Jackson stood, and was swinging himself up towards the window.

The four-fingered machine smashed through the window and swung baboon-like up on to the roof of the building. Running now, on his knuckles, the noise from the roofs of the metal buildings was incredible. If Jackson had wanted to keep a low profile, he had certainly chosen the wrong robot for the job. *Fist* bounded across roofs, flinging himself between buildings like some kind of mechanical free-runner, in an attempt to get to *Tread*.

'What d'you think *Fist* is going to do?' It was Brooke. 'Box their little ears? Leave this to me and *Punk*!'

The revolving swarm would have cut *Tread* in two if *Punk* had arrived a nanosecond later. The spiked wrecking ball slammed into the spiralling halo above *Tread*.

'Strike!' shouted Brooke, as all ten of the robots were scattered like skittles.

But in his contact with the swarm, one of *Punk*'s rotors was severed clean off and, try as she might, Brooke could not prevent him from spinning out of control. Brooke was struggling to regain control when he hit the windscreen of Yakimoto's helicopter, crashing straight though its transparent polycarbonate and burying two of his spikes in the pilot's seat.

Outside the helicopter, several more of Lear's tiny flying globes had assembled, buzzing manically around the shards of broken cockpit like flies round a carcass, before flowing in through the hole left by *Punk* and attaching themselves magnetically to his metal shell.

'There's no way of stopping them!' shouted Brooke. 'They're trying to scalp *Punk*!' Her response was as instant and instinctive as a block from a black belt. She flicked her phone and *Punk*'s power pack discharged a huge flash-current through all of his spikes – in one instant and surge. The small robots clinging to *Punk* were instantly fried, becoming useless pieces of melted plastic and circuitry by the time they hit the floor of the helicopter cockpit.

'Is *Punk* OK?' Jackson asked hurriedly.

'He's not going to win any aerobatics competitions anytime soon,' said Brooke, attempting to drive *Punk* back out of the cockpit. 'But he's still got some fight left in him!'

'Good!' said Jackson. 'Cos I think they're coming for me!'

CHAPTER 26

Jackson didn't have time to be scared as the robotic swarm buzzed in circles around the roof of his building.

'My guess is they're going for my satellite link on the roof first – to cut you out of the picture. Then they'll be coming for me!'

'Give me *Fist* then!' said Brook. 'And I'll set him on Lear!'

'No!' Jackson shook his head. 'There're too many of them. I need *Fist* to defend the satellite – chances are we're going to lose contact with each other soon and I need you to transfer a file from your tablet PC to *Punk*!'

'A file? What file?' asked Brooke.

'*Tug*'s personality!' yelled Jackson.

Jackson had a view from *Tread* of what was happening on the roof above him. *Tread*, who was still disabled by his own brake, remained in the twisted wreckage of an adjacent building, but his high-quality camera was show-ing Jackson a scene that was like some futuristic version of *King Kong*. *Fist* stood astride the satellite as the pint-sized swarm robots darted between swipes from his two free hands.

To observe Jackson at work with the phone in his hand would have been like watching a boxer fighting with his own shadow. Each distorted punch and abstract grapple that Jackson made was translated into hundreds of kilograms of load, compression and thrust through *Fist*'s memory metal muscles. When he connected with one of the balls, he hit it out of the park and it never came back, but overall the swarm was winning. Several of the diminutive machines had already struck the satellite on the roof above Jackson and, with them now beginning to circle in equilateral formation, Jackson wasn't confident of it being online for much longer.

'Come on, Brooke,' he cried. 'I need that file. I think we're going to lose the connection between us, any second now!'

'I'm working on it,' Brooke replied urgently, her voice fading intermittently as electromagnetic energy from the spinning swarm interfered with the delicate satellite data connection between the Canadian hut and her hijacked Wi-Fi Max antennae on Martha's Vineyard. 'Transfer is complete, Daddy-o!' she yelled triumphantly a few seconds later. '*Punk* is going to be as mad as a wet hen when he gets his old pal's mean side!'

No sooner had Brooke finished her sentence than the

flash of a laser pulsed overhead and all connection between the two friends was lost.

Worse still, one of the intensely hot beams from the swarm had caught *Fist*'s primary power unit. Three of his hands were twitching nervously and, despite all Jackson's efforts to recover him, he slipped off the roof and collapsed in a trembling, twisted heap.

Jackson could think of only one course of action – he ran outside, shouting.

The first ball-shaped machine that got in his way felt the force of his boot. Then the glowing red eyes of another eleven swarm machines turned towards him and Jackson began running harder than he had ever run before.

The air was so cold that it burned when Jackson took desperate mouthfuls as he ran. He rushed between two garages. The snow was blinding and it wasn't until he saw the edge of the mine at the end of the aisle he was running down that Jackson realized he was boxed in.

The swarm fanned out in a sickle shape, throat height, their red lights blazing.

So this is it! thought Jackson, as he cowered before the spiralling swarm. *Whatever Lear and Yakimoto's game is – they win. I lose.* He gulped down a freezing lungful of air that he feared might be his last.

The whole swarm shot forwards and Jackson closed his eyes, bracing himself for death. But to his amazement nothing happened.

Jackson swung round to see that all of the spherical swarm robots had shot straight past him. Four gunmen, the two from the entrance and Yakimoto's bodyguards, now stood before the swarm robots, spread out in defensive positions.

Jackson dived for cover as bullets from their automatic weapons started to fly. But the battle was short-lived. In a second the swarm formed up over the heads of the men and, pooling energy from each other, detonated a wave of sub-audible sound. Jackson recognized the signs of Lear's infamous Bass Bomb as the pressure wave emanating from the swarm hit the four men, causing them to drop their weapons and double up in pain. As the men fell to the frozen ground, the waves of the low-frequency oscillations vibrated through Jackson's stomach, making him vomit instantly.

Unlike the men who still lay on the ground, their bodies contorted in agony, Jackson hadn't taken the full force of the Bass Bomb, and after a few seconds he was able to pick himself up off the ice. He was physically exhausted and chilled to the bone, and felt like any attempt to move would make him spew. But if he thought he was due a respite, he was mistaken. Through the blizzard, from the path leading up from the mine, Jackson could see a shape emerging. He could hardly believe his eyes as the figure of Yakimoto emerged from the edge of the mine, seated inside one of the white powerlifters.

Now that the fearsome-looking white machine was upright, Jackson could see it was a robotically assisted heavy-lifting tool that encased its operator inside a steel skeleton and an armoured glass bubble. Jackson cowered down in the snow and watched as Lear's robots regrouped, changing the shape of their swarm into a densely packed dot. Yakimoto swung his machine's powerful rock-crushing arms in an attempt to swat the flying robot.

Jackson couldn't believe what he was seeing – a fight between Lear's machines and a mechanically enhanced Yakimoto. It made no sense to him at all. Weren't the two men in this criminal heist together?

A blinding pulse of white light burst from the circular swarm. Jackson recognized it as another of Lear's signature non-lethal weapons that Brooke and Jackson had used on the MeX robots – the Dazzler.

Yakimoto's machine was engulfed in a surge of electricity, dancing along and disabling its big white robotic legs and arms. But as Jackson's own eyesight slowly recovered from the harsh, glaring light, he noticed that the thick glass dome round the machine's Japanese operator had darkened to absorb the light. *Probably some sort of sunlight protection screen*, thought Jackson.

The lifter seemed to be limping a little now, as it carried Yakimoto towards Jackson. His gut was throbbing as he stumbled back between the buildings in a feeble attempt to escape the man-machine that moved relentlessly towards him. Out of nowhere, Lear's HEMTT vehicle emerged through the driving snow. Yakimoto must have seen the fast-moving object at the last second, as Jackson saw the lifter spring into the air like a white tiger to land on top of the moving truck.

Lear's truck slammed into the base of a crane, the force of the impact causing its articulated back section to buckle where it joined the driver's cabin. Yakimoto in his lifter moved quickly over the roof of Lear's camouflaged white vehicle, pursued by the swarm.

Once the powerlifter reached the back section of the truck it took just seconds for its powerful claws to mangle Lear's antennae arrays, smash his power supplies and rip out banks of batteries. The effect on the robotic horde was instantaneous and catastrophic. The entire swarm dropped from the sky.

Jackson felt a flood of relief when the burning red eyes in each of the robot balls slowly extinguished as they lay motionless on the frozen ground.

He desperately wanted to flee the scene of the fight, but was mesmerized by the spectacle of Yakimoto's muscular machine as it stomped along the top of Lear's vehicle towards the driver's cabin. Here were the two men he had travelled thousands of kilometres to find – locked in mortal combat. Jackson watched, rooted to the spot, as the lifter's talon ripped the driver-side door clean off Lear's eight-wheeler and plucked a struggling figure from the driving seat.

The silhouette of the lifter looked like a mechanical T-Rex, with its prey struggling helplessly in its jaws, as Yakimoto carried the pathetic figure of Devlin Lear towards the lip of the gaping diamond mine.

Jackson watched, horrified, as Lear was tossed over the precipice like a rag doll.

CHAPTER 27

Jackson felt something jabbing into the small of his back.

He turned round to see the fat, squat figure of the man he'd heard Mr Yakimoto refer to as Mr Botha.

'Walk!' he said, jamming his pistol harder into Jackson's spine.

Yakimoto had turned his lifter from the mine's edge and it was striding towards Jackson and the foreman.

The glass bubble hissed as it slid backwards.

For Jackson, the inescapable truth was that he was face to face with the man who'd caused so much pain and misery in his life – and there was nothing he could do to give him his just deserts. One wrong move and the gun in his back would go off.

'You and that other worm think you can come to my mine and steal my diamonds,' Yakimoto hissed. 'Tell me how you heard about my latest find, or you'll go the same way as your partner!'

'What are you talking about? Lear is your partner, not mine!' Jackson said wearily, still not quite understanding what he had just seen. 'I know all about the diamond deal the two of you struck.'

Yakimoto looked at Mr Botha and the two men burst out laughing. 'I have no *deal* with the snivelling scar-faced fool I just tossed to his death – whoever he was!' He strode forward, scooping Jackson up in the arms of the lifter.

'Tell me what you know, or I'll crush you where you stand!' Yakimoto touched the controls of the lifter and the talons that gripped Jackson's thighs clenched. The pressure was intense, but Jackson was determined not to give Yakimoto the satisfaction of him showing his pain. Then, just as Jackson felt his legs might crush under the force of the lifter's steel grip, he spotted one of Lear's dead spherical robots on the ground.

'I will only ask you one more time before I send you the same way as your friend – how did you know about my diamond discovery?'

'What diamond discovery?' shouted Jackson. 'I don't know what you're talking about!'

Yakimoto turned the lifter towards the icy precipice, and every movement sent fresh waves of pain into Jackson's body. Struggling to drag his phone from his pocket, Jackson tried to ignore the pain and focus on sending *Punk* a message: 'FTCH BLL'.

'OK, let me go,' Jackson pleaded. He needed vital seconds before he was crushed to death. 'I'll tell you everything.'

Yakimoto released the lifter's grip on Jackson and he dropped to the ground. Wasting no time, Jackson immediately spun round and grabbed Lear's defunct tennis-ball-sized robot, throwing it, cleanly, inside the cockpit of the lifter just as *Punk* shot out of the damaged helicopter, his spikes extending and retracting in an intricate matrix that had him moving along the ground towards Jackson and Yakimoto at incredible speed. Moments from reaching them, *Punk* bounced into the air. As he flew, each of his sharp spikes extended, all twelve reaching full extension in less than two microseconds.

Punk embedded himself into the lifter at shoulder height, one of his spikes piercing straight through Yakimoto's right cheek. He dropped into the cockpit cavity, spiking cables and electronics and human flesh at random as he searched doggedly for the ball that was rattling around somewhere inside.

As Mr Botha opened fire on *Punk*, Jackson took his chance – and ran.

Bullets from Botha's pistol ricocheted off the metal huts either side of Jackson as he half ran, half slid, on the icy ground, before he made it round one of the structures.

Jackson kept running, zigzagging between the garages and huts until he came across *Tread*. He tried to wrench the heavy wheel-bot from the debris of the building in which he was buried, but before he could free him he heard the cocking of a weapon. It was Botha again.

Jackson spun round. *Tread* pivoted on the spot, shooting a dart from the centre of its hub.

Tread had transmitted a wireless surge of electricity between his main power cell and the metal barb in Mr Botha's leg before the man even knew his skin had been pierced.

Botha let out a bloodcurdling scream and dropped his weapon as his muscles were paralysed by the flow of electricity. When it finished, he just lay on the ground whimpering. But at that moment his moans were drowned by the sound of beating helicopter blades. Jackson ran towards the helicopter pad to find Yakimoto in the cockpit of his helicopter as its rotors spooled up.

Luckily, Jackson slipped and fell to the ground, as a spray of bullets left the shattered cockpit and came in his direction.

Dragging himself to his feet, Jackson looked into the whirlwind of frozen, granular snow that was whipped up as the helicopter rose. He could see the bloodied face of Yakimoto, sneering at him through the smashed cockpit glass.

The helicopter continued to rise – until it was swallowed by the white sky.

The snow drove harder than ever against Jackson's face as he attempted to recover *Punk* from inside the frame of Yakimoto's powerlifter. As he scrabbled to get a grip with agonizingly cold hands, he thought he heard a whimper coming from the edge of the diamond mine.

The snowstorm was horizontal now, driven by an angry wind, as Jackson ventured towards the edge of the massive hole.

Through the white-out he could just make out the form of a person, clinging to a thin sliver of ice on the sheer rock face.

'Help me! Help me, Jackson!' It was the voice of Lear, drifting up from the churning mist.

Jackson edged gingerly down towards Lear. He could hardly believe what he was looking at – a beaten and bloody Devlin Lear balanced helplessly on a brittle, icy ridge, a swirling white cavity beneath him.

Jackson took his phone from his pocket. He held it up and snapped a mugshot of Lear's panic-stricken face. It was the evidence he needed to exonerate all of them.

'Why would I ever help you again?' Jackson shouted into the abyss.

'Because I'm Mr Pope,' spluttered Lear. 'Because, Jackson, I'm your father.'

Jackson was stunned. For a moment he said nothing – then rage bubbled up.

'You utter madman,' Jackson bellowed. 'You're not my father. How can you be?'

One of the legs that Lear had jammed into the ice slipped, and for a second Jackson thought the man would fall as he struggled desperately to find a crevice to hold on to. Lear cried out in pain and Jackson noticed that one of the hands clinging to the rock face was twisted and broken.

'I came here for the same reason you did, Jackson,' he cried. 'To catch Yakimoto. To make him pay for what he did to us! The diamonds. The reactor. I needed a way to catch his attention. I knew I could lure him here if pure blue diamonds were found in his mine.'

Jackson stared down at Lear, dumbfounded.

'Because he killed your mother, Jackson,' Lear continued. 'Yakimoto killed the only woman I ever loved.'

Jackson struggled to find the denial he desperately needed, but it evaded him. He thought about the photos of Mr Pope – about the face he had never quite been able to see. It all made a horrible kind of sense.

'But . . . what about the money?' shouted Jackson.

'I won't pretend I wasn't trying to extort money from the black-haired assassin Yakimoto,' Lear hissed. 'But the diamonds, Jackson. They're radioactive! Even now, as he flies away with them, he has no clue the stones are rotting him from the outside in.'

Without warning, the ice supporting Lear's feet cracked and he slipped.

'Aargh!' Only one foot was left on the crumbling ledge, with the fingers of one frozen, bloodstained hand jammed in a crack in the ice.

'But Mr Pope died!' Jackson's words echoed in the pit

as he tried to understand the truth about his parentage after weeks of torment over the mystery.

'I spent four years as a captive of Yakimoto's gang, hidden away in a forest camp deep in Japan. Even my own government didn't come looking for me as they thought I was dead. When eventually I managed to escape and make it back to England, I made myself a new identity so Yakimoto wouldn't hunt me down. He doesn't know who I really am.'

Suddenly Yakimoto's denials all made sense to Jackson. He really hadn't known who he was dealing with. Jackson glared furiously at Lear – at least he'd had the option to escape Yakimoto. His mother hadn't.

Lear's voice was strained as he struggled to hold on. 'That's when I found out that your mother had a child. You, Jackson. You were three years old. I couldn't make contact with your mother as I was worried Yakimoto's men might be on my trail and I didn't want to put her in any more danger. But I watched you from afar, Jackson, as you grew. I was, after all, trained by the same people your mother worked for and I used those skills to keep track of your progress. Over the years my business dealings made me a very rich man and enabled me to set up MeX. Through MeX, we finally met.'

The wind blew so hard on to the exposed ridge that Lear's hand slipped. Again he was able to recover it, but

Jackson could see he didn't have much more strength left in him.

'It doesn't make sense,' Jackson shouted. 'Why target the MIT reactor? Why kidnap me?'

'I may have been looking out for you, Jackson,' Lear cried, 'but my paternal instincts don't extend to that sanctimonious Professor English. It was his network that allowed you and that strange daughter of his to ruin MeX and turn me into a wanted man. Goulman and the reactor were my revenge against him.'

'But you left me tied up in the tunnels under the campus. I could have died in that reactor explosion!' replied Jackson.

'The tunnels were the safest place to be when my bomb went off. I had you picked up and left down there to guarantee your safety, Jackson.'

Lear started to slip. This time, his hand slid out of the crack in the ice.

'Hold on!' shouted Jackson, leaning out over the edge to grab Lear's hand. But all Jackson managed to clutch was a handful of the man's sleeve before the material started to rip.

'No!' Jackson couldn't let this happen. Not now – there were still so many things he needed to know.

The wind was blasting, the hole below roaring up at them. A frightened Lear looked at Jackson. 'I'm sorry, son,' he said. Then his coat sleeve ripped and he fell, his body consumed by the snowy chasm.

And as Jackson lay on the ground, staring open-mouthed into the abyss, a peaceful voice echoed through his head:

All things in the world are two.
Strong and weak, wise and unwise,
Friend and foe, father and son.

CHAPTER 28

Something inside Jackson was missing. It was the paranoia.

He was sitting in the window of Cyber Republic. Brooke was late, as usual, but things were looking up. He hadn't even needed to ask: his Coke had been waiting for him when he'd reached the checkout – a stack of 10.6 ice cubes floating in the brown-black liquid.

Across the street he could see the Cambridge Bicycle Shop beside which he'd once thought a sinister black van had waited. As it had turned out, he'd been right. That was partly why he was no longer scared – he knew the truth. He knew who his real father was. He knew his father was dead and that he hated him for the chaos he'd wrought. But he also knew that, even though Lear's greed and arrogance had wrecked too many lives, this man – who he still saw in recurring nightmares, falling into the snowy abyss – was the very reason that Jackson had had his mother in his life. And he was grateful for that, even for the short time he'd shared with her.

The FBI *had* come for Jackson. But thanks to the evidence Brooke had shown her local sheriff, it was a rescue mission rather than a manhunt. They'd also come for Goulman. They found him via a number of money transfers from an account they traced to Lear. Jackson hadn't ever needed to show them the picture on his phone to prove Lear's existence. Lear had incriminated himself and so Jackson deleted it. He knew who Lear was to him – he didn't need the photo.

The FBI's initial investigation had uncovered evidence that Lear had employed Goulman since before his faked death and that he had paid J.P.'s assistant over two million dollars to spy on Brooke, J.P. and Jackson. Brooke had taken that betrayal hard, but found some solace in the circumstances of Ghoul's capture. A Columbian coastguard found his yacht floating in the Pacific, stripped of everything and savaged by fire. Goulman himself had been beaten to within an inch of his life. He'd been attacked by pirates.

Yakimoto had so far evaded capture.

At first Jackson had tried to push Yakimoto from his mind, but in the weeks since the Canadian expedition information from the twins had revealed that he had made it back to Japan. Yakimoto might be alive, but the fear that had stalked Jackson since he'd gone against Lear, over a year ago, was no longer with him. Yakimoto didn't scare him; he made his blood boil. The rage Jackson felt towards the man who had killed his mother had also given him a new source of strength. Jackson had found himself fantasizing about what he would do if he came face to face with Yakimoto for a second time. His favourite idea saw him cleaving Yakimoto in two with one of WizardZombie's Enchanted Thunderfury Broadswords.

Brooke flashed into the cafe and jumped into the seat beside Jackson's.

'Come on then, tell me, did you hear back from Singer yet?' she asked excitedly.

'Yes, I did!' said Jackson.

'Tell me what he said already! Did we win?'

'I haven't opened the email yet; I thought I'd wait until you got here,' he answered.

With everything that had happened, Jackson had forgotten all about Singer's Artificial Intelligence competition, but Brooke hadn't. No sooner had Jackson arrived back in Boston, and Brooke had been entirely sure that he was OK, than she started pestering him about sending their data to the professor.

Jackson had made several alterations to the lines of raw code to hide the true identities of *Punk* and *Tug*, not to mention some of their defensive capabilities. But the two complementary personality profiles were there, with the idea that Jackson hoped might clinch it for them – the text-message interface.

Jackson used his phone to bring up the professor's

email. For a moment he just sat and read the words that seemed almost printed on the shiny white surface of the phone, then he started to shake his head despairingly.

Brooke's shoulders drooped. She was clearly very disappointed.

Suddenly Jackson beamed a big smile. 'I'm just kidding. It says we won!'

'I don't believe it!' said Brooke, bubbling over with excitement. 'I've actually won something! I am a winner!' Brooke jumped up and did a tiny jig beside her chair. 'Do we get a trophy? Tell me we get a trophy!'

'If you want a trophy, Brooke, I'm sure I can organize something,' said Jackson, grinning.

'Anyway, listen up, I've been thinking. I've got a new idea for a robot interface!' Her eyes were blazing with excitement. 'Mind control!'

'Sounds like a plan,' said Jackson. 'Let's do it!'

● EPILOGUE

Japan

The expensive hotel suite sat high above Akihabara, otherwise known as Electric Town.

It didn't matter how many times Mr Kojima looked at the Tokyo skyline, he never grew tired of it. Every colour imaginable was here, infused with electric light, drawing the outlines of buildings, which, in his opinion, were as beautiful as any of Japan's mountains, forests and lakes.

Mr Kojima squinted as the rest of his family arrived, the flashbulbs that accompanied them bouncing off the floor-to-ceiling glass window. Three of the security guards he employed pressed against the doors and squeezed the press and autograph hunters out.

He leaned forward in a deep uncurving bow, his eyes never leaving his five children.

'Sit down, little ones,' said the man's elegant wife, pulling back chairs for her three youngest, and motioning the older Kojima twins to sit round the large table that dominated the centre of the room.

Mr Kojima waited for them all to settle – and then a little while longer as was his way, until they were completely silent.

'Tonight is a proud night for our family,' he said, raising his chin. 'The twins have won another great victory.' Everyone round the glass table, which included the three six-year-old identical sisters, clapped politely.

Mr Kojima looked down and locked the twins in a serious stare.

'As the winners of Japan's most coveted professional computer-gaming tournament,' he continued, 'we now have the noble responsibility of carrying the Kojima family name with pride and dignity. Tonight's tournament win may feel like the crowning achievement of the last few years, but it is only the beginning. Before us all is a lifetime in which people will look to us for inspiration and leadership.'

Master Kojima couldn't help but let out a stunted snigger at the idea that he, a ten-year-old gamer, was some kind of role model for *inspiration and leadership*. In turn, his sister spat out a single subdued laugh.

All their father needed to do was widen his eyes, and the twins fell instantly silent again.

'I have reserved a restaurant for us and some of your friends.'

A buzz of excitement shot around the room.

'As we make our way there,' Mr Kojima continued, 'I ask that you conduct yourselves with dignity. All of Japan will be watching.' He then nodded and the family scraped back their chairs and moved towards the door.

The family scurried along the hotel corridor and into the lift, two thickset suited guards at the front and one behind – enough to keep the handful of photographers and diehard gaming fans at bay.

When they reached the lobby, it was a different affair. From the moment they left the lift, throngs of young people and paparazzi stuck everything from notepads to full-sized digital TV cameras in their faces. The twins smiled and tried to scribble on the pads and scraps of paper thrust before them as they were ushered along.

With their bodyguards carving a way through the crowd, the family finally reached the pavement outside, where a stretch limousine was waiting for them.

Suddenly three tiny metallic discs rolled on to the ground between them and the car and instantly began to smoke. Everyone around the car started coughing and choking. Mr Kojima and his bodyguard struggled to push his wife and children into the waiting car – which by now was revving hard. But, unexpectedly, his wife flew backwards out of the car, knocking into the triplets, the four of them landing awkwardly on the pavement.

The car, with the Kojima twins inside, spun its wheels

and raced away. Mr Kojima and the bodyguards ran down the road after it, in a pointless attempt to catch up.

On the back seat of the car, Master and Miss Kojima struggled to open the doors and windows.

A smartly dressed man in the passenger seat turned to a driver the twins didn't recognize and laughed. He then leaned towards the twins with his hand inside his suit jacket.

'I suggest you both sit quietly and listen carefully,' said the middle-aged Japanese man calmly. 'You have a choice. You can both take a pill I have prepared that will render you harmlessly unconscious for the duration of our journey, or I can knock you both unconscious.' He slid a pistol out of his inside pocket then spun it round so he was holding it butt forward, like a hammer.

The man's mouth arched into a broad smirk before he coughed loudly.

As Master Kojima held his trembling sister close to him, he could just make out a neatly stitched scar on the man's right cheek, most of which was covered by the long wisps of jet-black hair that framed his face.

Acknowledgements

Thank you to Claire and my children who yet again had to lose me from their adventures during the writing of *Atomic Storm*. And to Rich23 who is my only friend with a number in his name. Thanks to the real Atticus – who I met over tea in Cambridge, Massachusetts, and who ended up showing me every inch of MIT.

I must also thank all the cafe owners who didn't charge for laptop juice while I sat writing for days on end – principally everyone at Zoran's Deli.

I am enormously grateful to my agents, Luigi and Debbie, for believing me when I said I was a children's author. And my heartfelt thanks, plus a big high-five, go to the Puffin gang. I feel privileged to work with such a dedicated and talented group of people – especially my editor, Lindsey Heaven, who is as divine as her really cool surname suggests.

Most of all, thanks to everyone who has read the first Dot.Robot book and eagerly awaits the second in the series – that means all of you who have been to the Dot.

Robot Roadshow events in schools and festivals and my followers on Twitter – you make it all worthwhile.

I would also like to acknowledge a website called www.firstpeople.us where I found a quote from the real Eagle Chief (Letakos-Lesa) Pawnee that inspired the fictional American Indian in this book and the words Jackson reads in his book.

> WARNING!

THERE'S MORE ACTION TO COME IN

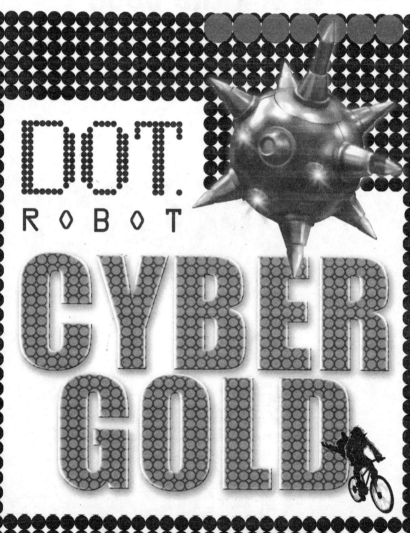

DOT.
R O B O T

CYBER
GOLD

> FEBRUARY 2011